A
Harlequin
Romance

OTHER

Harlequin Romances

by MARY WIBBERLEY

Many of these titles are available at your local bookseller or through the Harlequin Reader Service.

For a free catalogue listing all available Harlequin Romances, send your name and address to:

HARLEQUIN READER SERVICE,
M.P.O. Box 707, Niagara Falls, N.Y. 14302
Canadian address: Stratford, Ontario, Canada N5A 6W4

or use order coupon at back of book.

THAT MAN BRYCE

by

MARY WIBBERLEY

HARLEQUIN BOOKS   TORONTO
WINNIPEG

Original hard cover edition published in 1975
by Mills & Boon Limited

SBN 373-01935-1

Harlequin edition published December 1975

Printed in Canada

1935

CHAPTER ONE

KIM was frightened. In the distance a child cried, but it wasn't that which had frightened her. It was the utter stillness, the loneliness—the waiting. Where was he? He should be here.

All was quiet again, the child had stopped crying, the train had vanished round a bend in the track so that even the comforting tail light, her last link with civilisation, was no longer to be seen. The little Austrian station was in darkness. No ticket collector, no other passengers. Nothing. One solitary light cast its icy blue glow over the huddle of black buildings. Kim's breath froze as it left her mouth, and the air stung her cheeks with tiny needles. She pushed her hands more deeply into the pockets of her winter coat and began to walk. Anything was preferable to standing still and freezing.

But where *was* he? She could see houses beyond the station, some with lights at the windows, and in a few minutes she would have to go and ask if she could telephone, because perhaps he hadn't received her telegram. The darkness had a tense quality to it, a waiting air, as if it knew of her deception...

'Excuse me——' the voice was deep, and came from behind her shoulder so that she whirled round, heart beating fast. She had heard no sound.

'Yes?' The heartbeats subsided and became normal as she saw the man standing so quietly before her. He was tall and broadly built, but that was all she could see, for it was too dark.

'I am looking for a man,' the stranger said. 'Is there anyone with you?'

'No, I'm alone.' But she was beginning to wonder if he had come from Gordon—and was expecting her brother after all. 'Have you come to meet someone?' A ridiculous question, and he was slightly unnerving her because he was so big, so powerful-looking, and there was no one else in earshot, no one at all. She moved ever so slightly away, almost unaware of it herself until he said:

'You are quite safe. And yes, I have come to meet someone.' His accent was neither French nor German nor anything she could recognise, yet tantalisingly familiar.

There was an edge of mockery in those first words. Almost amused. Kim tilted her chin up. She might as well find out now, before she froze. 'Someone called Jack Dalby?' She sensed his puzzlement even before he answered.

'Yes—but——?' The unspoken question hung in the air like icy needles.

'He's my brother. I've come in his place. I was expecting Gordon——'

A wordless exclamation, and even then something stirred within her, a faint unease at what she might be doing.

'I do not understand.' The deep voice sounded angry.

'It's quite simple really. Can you take me to Gordon? It's very cold here.' She was beginning to feel annoyed herself. Who was this man? Who did he think he was? Any explanations were due to Gordon, whom she knew, not some dark stranger she had just encountered on a deserted railway station.

'It might be better.' He cut off the words as if he too had no wish to stay. 'Where is your luggage?'

'Over there.' She pointed and walked away. Her two cases were heavy, but he picked them up as if they were made of balsa wood, and strode back.

'Come with me.'

The sleek dark Mercedes waited throbbing silently. No wonder she had heard nothing. A few soft flakes of snow drifted down as she watched him put the cases in the boot, slam it closed and then open her passenger door. 'It was not locked,' he said dryly, and she felt herself redden at the implication that perhaps she was too lazy to open it herself. She slid in, biting back any retort. Men didn't usually have this effect on her, but then she had never met one like this before. Even though she had not seen him properly yet, there was a sense of overwhelming power emanating from him and she began to wonder who he was. Servant, chauffeur? Somehow she knew he was neither of those.

She watched him as he swung into the driver's seat. The interior light flashed only briefly in those few seconds, but she caught her breath. Dark, handsome, unsmiling features, and his hair as black as night. Then, instead of starting off, he turned to her. 'So,' he said. 'Now it is not cold. Now you can tell me why you are here.'

'I can't see you,' she said, absurdly. He flicked a

switch and the light came on again, warm yellow flooding the large vehicle.

'Perhaps that is better, yes?'

'A little.' She swallowed. 'Where is Gordon?'

'He had to go to Vienna. He asked me to meet you—no, not you, but your brother, of course.' He made it sound as if he didn't believe anything she might say.

'Vienna? But I've just come from there,' she said, dismayed. If only she had known!

'Perhaps. But his trip was sudden. You had probably already started on the train by then. And I do not think, Miss Dalby, that you have answered my question yet.'

'I don't know who you are,' she answered.

'Perhaps you would like to see my passport?' He reached into an inner pocket of his coat, as if searching. 'Then perhaps you will feel free to speak, yes?'

His arrogance stung her. 'Just a name will do, thank you,' she retorted.

'My name is Bryce Drovnik. I am a friend of Gordon Hillaby's, but I have never heard of *you*.'

'Nor I of you,' she answered swiftly.

'No? But is that so surprising?' He had the disconcerting habit of constantly questioning her. It threw her slightly off balance. How much easier it would all have been if Gordon had been there. Then she realised something, and, ignoring his question, said:

'But—if Gordon's away, where are you taking me?'

'To the house where he is staying. Where else?'

She took a deep breath. She was tired after the plane flight, and too little sleep the previous night, because she had been going over everything repeatedly in her mind, wondering if her impulse to go was a stupid one. She didn't know exactly why Gordon wanted Jack, only that he was to take his scuba diving suit, that it was urgent, and that the less anyone else knew, the better. And now this big, aggressive, *questioning* man had turned up, and although it might not be the last straw, it wasn't far from it.

'Then please may we go?' she asked, politely, carefully.

'Yes.' The engine throbbed more loudly and they moved forward in an instant. Kim sat back in the comfortable seat and closed her eyes. It would soon be all right, of course it would. Gordon would make it so when he returned . . .

'Wake up, Miss Dalby. We are here.' Kim sat up, blinked, opened her eyes. She had fallen asleep. Unthinkable, but true. She had not thought she would be able to relax sufficiently with *him* to do so, but she had. She smiled slightly to herself at the thought, but he must have caught it and she saw the merest flicker of a frown cross his face as he stood waiting impatiently at the open door of the car.

She slid out, resisting the desire to have a good stretch. The cold air struck her even more forcefully after the cushioned warmth of the car, and she looked towards Gordon's house. And took a deep breath. Wow! she thought. A white mansion, ablaze with light, and if there wasn't a good story here, her name wasn't Katherine Emma Dalby. A tingle of anticipation touched her spine. Never mind this unwelcoming, aggressive creature. Gordon was the one who counted, and she had always been able to twist him nicely round her little finger, ever since the age of seven when her father had brought him to the house to meet them all.

And at that thought she sobered slightly. It wasn't far from here that her father had been killed ... Seven years ago, but there was still pain in memory, especially if one came suddenly, like that.

'Shall we go in?' she said quickly.

'Of course. I hoped you would want to. As you remarked at the station, it is rather cold to stand around.' It was there again, subtly veiled but potent—hard arrogance. He had expected to meet a man, her brother, but she had come instead, and he disliked the fact intensely. Hard luck, chum, Kim said inwardly, as they walked towards the welcoming lights of the house. I don't care if you are a woman-hater, I'm not out to impress *you*. You don't count. But there she was wrong.

The hot drink, the meal, the cheese and biscuits afterwards, they all made a difference to the atmosphere. She was sitting by a roaring log fire and the coffee pot was on a low table beside her so that all she had to do was reach out if she wanted another cup. Kim sat back in the easy chair, comfortable enough to fall asleep in if she wasn't careful. Bryce Drovnik had vanished—she wondered if it was to telephone someone, but she was too hungry to care. A man had brought the food in to her, told her his name was Matthew, and her room was ready when she needed it. She had only to ring. At least he showed no surprise at her presence, and was very courteous and helpful.

Drovnik? Some middle European name, but from where? She still hadn't placed the accent, and it was annoying. She still hadn't had a proper look at him, either, having been too dazzled by lights and sudden warmth, and by the fact that she had actually *arrived*. Gordon wouldn't turn her away now, would he? Kim reached out for the coffee pot, luxuriating in the warmth of the silky rug beneath her nyloned toes. The faint click as the door opened, and then his voice:

'You have eaten sufficiently?' Cool; he didn't really care, but he was making an effort. And now she would see him properly. She half turned, and looked up, and her heart skipped a beat.

Bryce Drovnik was even bigger than she had first thought, broad-shouldered, built on the lines of some powerpacked athlete. The black-as-night hair was right. Tanned face, high-cheekboned, and square-chinned—not a man to cross, it would seem, not with that hawk-like nose, wide cruel mouth— and those eyes. Hypnotic eyes, difficult to see the colour, for they were deep-set under level brows, but they held hers in a hard cool glance as he repeated his question.

'Yes—thank you.' He moved, panther-like, towards the fire. And stood there looking down at her.

'I have phoned Gordon,' he said.

She would *not* let him frighten her. Did he ex-

11

pect panic at that remark?

'Did you? I would have spoken to him if I'd known,' she answered, and managed to smile sweetly at the man. It slid off him like water off a stone.

'You will be able to do so tomorrow, when he returns.' His tone implied that Gordon was only returning because she had arrived instead of Jack.

Kim took a deep breath. If she wasn't careful, she would lose her temper, and maybe that was what he wanted.

'Good,' she nodded. 'I've not seen him for ages. I was looking forward to seeing him tonight as a matter of fact. We have a lot to talk over.' Especially you, you arrogant beast, she added to herself.

'Yes, I'm sure you have. And then, no doubt, you will be on your way home again.' It was his turn to smile now, a deep crooked smile, showing white teeth—and hidden amusement. Kim fought to control her precarious temper.

'What—what do you mean?' she managed.

He shrugged. 'We wanted Jack to help us with—something——' she noted his hesitation before the word, 'and I do not think you can take his place.'

'Don't you? If it's anything to do with underwater diving I can. I've brought my suit, Mr Drovnik, and I'm as good as my brother.'

'You?' He didn't trouble to hide his disbelief.

'Yes.' Kim stood up slowly. She was at too much of a disadvantage down in that chair, and she was going to need all her wits with this one. 'You obviously haven't asked Gordon that question, or he would have told you. He taught us both—he and my father, years ago. I've served my apprenticeship underwater, you might say. And because Jack wasn't able to come, I'm here in his place, so as not to let Gordon down. It's as simple as that.' So put that in your pipe and smoke it, she mentally added.

'Simple? I wonder?' Bryce Drovnik smiled again, but with scarcely a trace of amusement. 'You see, there is one small point—and perhaps it should be mentioned now. Since his accident seven years ago, Gordon has been unable to venture in the water, let alone scuba dive. It is I who persuaded him to send for your brother. I who will be diving, not Gordon. I need a man to work with, not you, Miss Dalby. Forgive me if I seem rude, but I am not prepared to risk anything now, or to put it another way, I need a diving partner, someone who is prepared to pull his weight—not someone I need to keep a constant eye on.'

He expressed himself very clearly, she thought— and insultingly.

'Then you should know I'm not a fragile flower. I imagine you're looking for something underwater. Right?' At his faint nod, she went on crisply: 'And as you're such an *expert*'—she emphasised the word—'you should know that a woman is just as capable as a man when it comes to scuba diving. Water is a great leveller, if you'll pardon the expression.' Heavens, was he actually starting to smile?

'Miss Dalby, you have a persuasive tongue for such a young woman. However'—he shrugged eloquently, 'I am sorry, but I am not prepared to——'

'Test me!' she cut in. 'Then you'll see.'

'I do not understand.' The smile had been replaced by a frown.

'It's quite simple,' she spoke as if to a child. 'I have my scuba outfit with me. Are you scared I'll be better than you or something?'

He looked her up and down—slowly. Those eyes were dark green, pebbles under water, cold and appraising. But her words had had their effect, had reached him. 'No,' he said slowly, 'I am not scared. But I do not have time to waste——'

'You don't have much choice,' she rejoined sweetly. 'Jack isn't here, and he's not coming. He's in South America, as a matter of fact——'

And just then the phone rang from somewhere outside the room, a long shrill sound that silenced her words. Bryce Drovnik began to move towards the door. He wasn't angry—but he wasn't far away from it either.

'You have your wish, Miss Dalby. I will see you in the morning—after you have breakfasted. Goodnight. Ring for Matthew when you wish to go to your room.' And then he was gone, leaving only the lingering aftertaste of his powerful presence. Slowly Kim sat down again. She needed another cup of coffee. She hoped there was one. There was.

The crisp cold air made her draw her breath sharply as light flooded the room. A plump middle-aged woman stood by the open shutters, turned slowly and smiled at Kim.

'Good morning, miss. Would you like your breakfast up here?'

'Yes, please. Just a little toast and coffee, if you

14

don't mind.' And she smiled. Perhaps the test had already begun. It was dangerous to dive on a full stomach. 'Is Mr Drovnik up yet?'

'Yes, miss. He's gone down to the lake. He said to tell you—when you're ready, my husband will show you the way there.'

'Thank you. Are you Matthew's wife?'

'Yes, miss. Call me Ann,' she nodded briskly. 'I'll go and get your breakfast.'

'Wait—Ann. I'll have it after. Is Mr Drovnik dressed for diving?'

'He's in his wet suit, yes. Are you sure?'

'Yes, quite sure. Then I'll have an appetite. The meal last night was excellent. I'm still full.'

'Just as you like. There's a bell in the hall. Matt will take you.' Ann went out, and Kim looked round the bedroom she had occupied the previous night. She had never assumed that Gordon was so wealthy, but the evidence was all about her in the room and in the brief glimpses she had caught of the rest of the house on her arrival. The fitted wardrobes were in a soft cream wood, the carpet, so thick underfoot, in a matching shade, white walls —with pictures that couldn't be originals, could they? Because if they were they must be worth thousands. Kim crossed to one, to see it more clearly, and took in a deep breath. It was a Paul Klee, and it didn't look like a print—she turned to the drawing behind her bed. It couldn't be an original Rodin—but it was. So, she thought, I wonder what on earth we are searching for? And where does Bryce Drovnik fit into all this? But she would have to wait for the answers until Gordon came home.

Her wet suit was in her second suitcase, as yet untouched. She washed in the bathroom adjoining her room and, after donning her swimsuit, pulled on the black rubber outfit. She could not resist a peep in the long wardrobe mirror when she was dressed. Tall and slender-waisted as she was, the anonymous black of the suit could not hide the feminine curves, and in a strange way it only served to accentuate the cool beauty of her features, the small but determined chin, smoky blue green eyes, thickly lashed; pert mouth and nose. Kim grinned at herself. 'Vain hussy!' she chided. But she knew she looked good, and it would help, with *him*. Even though he appeared highly resistant to her so far.

Picking up her flippers, Kim went to the door and opened it. Matthew appeared at the first ring on the bell in the hall, and smiled at her.

'Morning, miss. I'll take you down to the lake. Mr Drovnik is already there.'

'Yes, your wife told me. Thank you, Matthew.'

The air was cool outside, but a warm sun would soon change that. Mountains soared effortlessly to the sky, white and cruel—but beautiful even so.

It was only to make conversation, as they made their way down the red-gravelled drive, crossed a lawn and went down into the woodland that Kim said: 'It's glorious here, isn't it? Have you been with Mr Hillaby long?'

'Pardon, miss?' Matthew looked at her, startled. 'Mr Hillaby?'

Kim wondered what she had said wrong. It had

16

been a perfectly innocent question ... 'You're mistaken, miss. Mr Hillaby is a guest here. The house is Mr Drovnik's.'

CHAPTER TWO

THE fact took a few seconds to digest, while Kim did some hasty mental arithmetic. Bryce Drovnik was her host, not Gordon. She couldn't take it in—not yet. And then the trees cleared, and she saw a vast expanse of shimmering water, and the puzzle was temporarily forgotten as she stood stock still to take it in, to absorb the sheer beauty of the lake that stretched for what seemed like miles and miles...

'You like it?' Matthew was watching her, amused. 'It takes your breath away, doesn't it?'

'It does,' she admitted. 'Oh, but it does!' Nobody moved near or in the water, but there was a boathouse, white-painted, green-shuttered, standing at the edge of the lake, and Matthew led her there.

And then she saw Bryce Drovnik, moving out towards them, and Matthew said: 'I'll get back to the house. Let us know when you want breakfast.' He gave an answering wave to the tall dark man standing silently now by the shingly shore, and turned to go back. Kim's heartbeat became erratic. Bryce Drovnik was dressed in a wet suit, similar to her own, but differently filled. Very different.

Broad shoulders, sleekly clad now, lean-waisted and hipped and long-legged—he looked very formidable, almost forbidding.

'Good morning,' he nodded briefly. 'You have breakfasted?'

So it was a test. A challenge of any kind was stimulating to Kim. She smiled. 'Good morning. No, I prefer to dive on an empty stomach. Don't you?'

A small smile, that merely quirked the corners of his mouth was the only acknowledgement. 'Of course. Then you are ready?'

'Yes.' She could see into the boatshed now. The boat was a powerful-looking craft, although small, and ready for launching into the water. On a bench were two sets of compressed air tanks. Bryce Drovnik went over and lifted the first. They were heavy, clumsy on land but almost a part of you once under the water, but he carried it easily over to her and she turned away, ready for him to help her on with it. Teamwork was the keyword in this kind of occupation. At least he didn't expect the impossible—yet.

'Right?'

'Yes, thank you.' A tingle of excitement at the unknown was already in her blood. The air tanks were in place, securely attached, the mouthpiece dangling from the end of the tube, and in a minute, when she had helped him with his air, she would fit the mask over her eyes and nose, and adjust them, and test that the air was coming through.

He watched her do this, calm and cold, a forceful figure who was only waiting for her to make a mistake... But she would not, she knew that, and as they waded into the water, a calmness, a certainty, came over her. The test had already begun, and let him try what he would, she was ready, and alert.

The lake was cold, of course, but in minutes the thin layer of water that would become trapped between skin and suit would be warmed by her body, acting as an insulation. The rubber flippers, so clumsy on land, were powerful propellers of the body, and when they were a distance away from the shore and he signalled to her, and dived down, she followed immediately, kicking upwards with her feet, going down into greeny-blue depths, relying solely on the compressed air now, under water.

It was a different world, shadowy, vague, at first, then as her eyes adjusted, becoming clearer. Beneath her the sandy lake bottom littered with stones and pebbles and graceful waving plants. Tiny fish panicked at their approach and darted away, and Bryce surged forward towards the deeper water, swimming powerfully, not looking back.

Kim followed, exhilarated now, in her true element, swimming with lithe grace that was perhaps deceptive, for she was strong as well. And Bryce Drovnik turned, lying as it were on his back in their new world, watching her. Eerie, because with the mask on, concealing his features, he was an almost sinister figure, a silent black enemy—Absurd! Kim chided herself for the thought. But a cold shiver touched her spine. She paused, to await his instructions, and he pointed and began to swim away again, not waiting. They came to rocks, jagged cruel rocks that rose from the lake bed, encrusted with tiny plants and a kind of moss, and a crab scuttled away, startled at their presence. Faint sunlight still filtered through the clear water greenly and made strange shadows. Bubbles rose to the surface, and Bryce paused, his flippers raising flurries of sand as they touched the lake bottom. Kim waited again. He pointed to the nearest rock, making a lifting motion with both arms.

So this is stage two, Kim thought wryly. Well, I asked for it! She swam slowly forward assessing the situation. He wanted her to move the rock. It would be impossible on land, she knew, but here everything was different, especially weight. And he intended seeing if she was capable—or if she was the 'fragile flower' she had so scornfully denied.

You didn't rush into anything here. You studied the situation first, and then decided. Kim swam round the jagged boulder slowly, touching it, pushing gently. It might have been embedded in concrete. She swallowed, took a deep breath, and the bubbles rose to the surface protestingly. A lever of some sort was needed. Without any kind of signal to the waiting man, she darted away, skimming the lake bed, searching until she found what she sought, a rusty piece of metal. Her heart lifted. That would do it, she knew—she *hoped*. It was barely two feet long, but solid enough, and she tested it with her hands as she swam triumphantly back to him and held it before the inscrutable mask.

He nodded. That was all. Did it signify approval?

You're in the right place, she thought, you're a

cold fish. But she no longer cared. Gently now, easing the metal stick under one side, pushing a smaller, loose rock, under the middle and then pressing down. The embedded rock shifted slightly, that was all. At least it wasn't set in concrete. She repeated this several times, and the sand swirled and settled again, and Bryce Drovnik waited, treading water gently, and Kim thought, what the hell am I doing this for? But she knew, she already knew. It was as much a test for herself as for him.

Then came the moment when she used all her strength, and the huge rock came free, and she pushed it over, and looked at the man. Slowly came the signal she had awaited. The thumbs-up sign—universal sign language of approval.

He pointed upwards. The next stage was here. Kim had estimated that they were about fifty to sixty feet underwater, and you didn't just swim directly to the surface, you took it nice and slowly so that the body could adjust to the difference in pressure. And he waited for her to go first. Which she did, and took her time, although now she was really hungry.

Gently swimming, kicking out lazily, going upwards, pausing, going again, until, just a few feet below the blinding surface, you waited, and breathed gently and slowly until it was safe to emerge.

The sun was warm and strong in the dazzlingly blue sky, and there wasn't a cloud to be seen anywhere. Kim swam until she felt shingle beneath the clumsy flippers, then waded in to shore, pulling the mask and mouthpiece off, taking in the heady mountain air, as exhilarating as champagne. She sat on a smooth flat rock and removed the flippers, and watched Bryce Drovnik do the same. Then he lifted off her air tanks and carried them into the boathouse.

'Breakfast now?' he said.

'Yes. I didn't know this was your house,' she said. She was not going to ask him how she had fared underwater. He would be waiting for her to do so, and she didn't intend to give him the satisfaction.

'No?' He shrugged, and it was almost as if he had added: 'So what?' The black hair dripped water, and he ran his fingers through it as if impatient. 'Does it matter to you?' he asked her.

'Of course. I thought I was coming to Gordon's house.'

'He is my partner. My home is his for as long as he wishes. He is a very good friend.'

Partner in what? She would ask Gordon when he returned. Oh, there were so many questions to ask him. 'When will he return?' she asked.

'Today. Then——' he paused; a faint shrug.

Kim didn't need to ask. She stood up. 'I'm hungry,' she said. 'May we go back?'

'Of course. You have rested?'

'I don't need a rest after swimming,' she responded pleasantly. A crooked smile was the only reply he gave her.

They began to walk towards the trees that screened the lake from the house. Kim's sandalled feet felt light. She could have run, so hungry was she. It must be this mountain air, she thought.

He walked beside her silently, thoughtful, secretive. A strange man, Kim was beginning to realise, unlike any she had ever met, and she had encountered many different types in her job. And at the thought of that, her footsteps faltered momentarily. Gordon knew what she did for her living—but this man did not. And what would happen when he found out? She might soon know. He had noticed the brief hesitation, for he gave her a shrewd sideways glance.

'I thought I had a pebble in my sandal,' she said. He was too sharp for her liking—in more ways than one. It might be better if she could talk privately to Gordon first.

'Yes?' he said. 'They can be painful.' But he didn't care, not really. The house came into view as they emerged from the trees into the sunlight again. It really was beautiful, and elegant, and up one wall at the back a spreading patch of ivy lent colour to the brilliant whiteness.

The roof was of red pantiles, the open shutters were green, and many were the windows. And it belonged to this man. Yet she had never heard of him, never read anything about him, and that was unusual in her work.

Two grey shapes suddenly appeared, and hurtled towards them at speed. 'Stand still,' Bryce commanded her, and she obeyed, freezing to the spot. Because when two giant alsatians seem intent on reaching you in seconds there's not much else you can do, thought Kim, quashing panic. They reached Bryce, who said quietly: *'Podozhdite!'* They subsided and lay, panting gently at his feet, two powerful beasts who at one word of command from their master, had obeyed instantly. Kim looked at him with unwilling respect. He spoke again to them and they rose and came towards her wagging apologetic tails as he talked softly to them. A tingle ran up Kim's spine as she held out her hand for them to sniff. Not of fear—but of recognition.

She should have known before, should have realised where he came from. But now, as he spoke in his own tongue, she did.

'What are their names?' she asked.

'Boris and Valery,' he answered. 'They guard the grounds at night. Don't worry, they will not attack you now they have been introduced.'

'I know. They are beautful animals. Did you bring them with you from Russia?'

There was a second of hard brittle silence, then he asked: 'Why do you ask that?'

She had done something wrong, but she didn't know why. There was a shuttered look to his face, a tightening of his jaw muscles, and, not for the first time, she felt frightened of him.

'I wondered,' she said slowly. 'That is all.'

'You speak the tongue?'

'A little. I've been there once.'

'Yes?' They began walking again, followed by the dogs, obediently trotting at Bryce's heels. 'So. And what other languages do you speak?'

Was he merely making conversation, or did he have a reason for asking? Kim began to feel confused. Oh, hurry up, Gordon, she thought. Where are you when I need you? 'French. German—

Spanish. I've travelled a lot. Why?' she asked bluntly.

'Because I like to know what kind of people I have in my house, that is why,' he answered calmly. 'Do you find that strange?' Hard voice, hard questions—hard man. Yet, sobering thought, he was her host.

'No. But I am an old friend of Gordon's—isn't that enough?' she answered, more quietly now.

'It should be. How strange that he should never have mentioned you, though,' he commented.

Kim felt a prickly surge of anger towards him, and keeping her voice calm with difficulty, said: 'You sound as if you think I'm an impostor or something. Would you like to see *my* passport?' This, remembering his own remark on meeting her.

'Why should I? Soon enough he will be here. Besides'—he looked down at her from his superior height—'I hardly feel in any danger from you.'

She ignored that, because at that moment, a vague memory had stirred at the back of her mind, and she tried desperately to retain it—but it was gone. A fleeting remembrance, disturbing, amorphous—and vanishing as quickly as it had come. An item in a newspaper, that was all—but something had triggered it off, she didn't know what. She looked back towards the lake, but it was hidden by trees now, and the memory, whatever it had been, had gone. She wondered if it would return.

It was late afternoon. Kim was restless, although she wasn't sure why. There was plenty to do, reading, walking, television, and as far as her material comforts were concerned the man Bryce Drovnik was an excellent host—even though indirectly. They had breakfasted together, and he had disappeared afterwards, saying he had a lot of work to do and would she excuse him?

She had, she reflected, hardly any choice. Ann had come in to clear the breakfast dishes away and told her that Mr Drovnik had said she was to show her the library, the television room, and anything else she might need.

'I'd like to phone home, if I may,' Kim told her. 'Is the village far?'

'But you can phone from here, miss,' Ann told her with a puzzled smile. 'He won't mind.'

'Are you sure?' Kim asked, momentarily fearful that he would come upon her as she dialled and take the telephone from her hands. Absurd, of course, but that was the way he got you.

'I'll ask him if you like,' Ann answered. 'Won't be a minute,' and she went out.

Kim wondered why an English couple were working for a Russian. Not impossible, but improbable somehow. Another question for Gordon, when he came.

She had phoned her grandmother and assured her of her safe arrival, and promised to write. Even as she spoke, she had to repress a smile. Anyone less like a grandmother was hard to imagine. Kim had in fact just caught her before she dashed off in her red Mini to coffee with two old friends. No old lady sitting at home worrying about her granddaughter at large in a foreign country, Florence Dalby had been instrumental in persuading Kim to take

Jack's place. 'Old Gordon will appreciate the joke,' she had assured Kim a few days previously, 'and give him my love, dear.'

Kim put the phone down at last, sensing that she was keeping her grandmother from her gossipy morning, and had heard a faint click as she did so. A tingle touched the back of her neck. Had Bryce Drovnik been listening in? Possibly—but why?

The memory of that came flooding back to Kim as she sat watching a sports programme on television. Saturday afternoon, and sport was sport the world over and she should be relaxing and enjoying it instead of worrying about things. She wasn't even sure why she was worrying. She was comfortable, there was a coffee pot beside her, replenished by the ever-watchful Ann only a few minutes before, there was a roaring fire in the grate, and a black cat slept happily at her feet. And any minute Gordon would be here.

But the faint click at the end of her conversation with her grandmother, and another fainter memory of coming back from the lake, refused to leave Kim's mind. She poured herself a cup of coffee, the cat stretched and yawned, and from outside there came the unmistakable whirr of a helicopter's blades, nearer and nearer, and louder ...

Kim went to the window, and outside was dusk, with stars beginning to shine in a cold frosty sky, but she didn't see them, only the huge mosquito-like creature overshadowing it all, sinking lower and lower, rotor blades click-clicking slower and slower, and stopping as it landed on a flat concrete strip at the back of the house. She stood at the window fascinated, saw a tall dark figure of a man leave the shadows of the house and walk towards the helicopter, saw the smaller figure stepping down awkwardly, then shaking hands ... Gordon!

She turned away from the window, wanting to go out, knowing she couldn't. But what would that man Bryce be saying to Gordon? She would soon know. Restlessly she walked back towards the fire, and the cat jumped up on the chair, purring loudly. Kim picked it up, a lovely creature wearing a red tartan collar, and began to stroke it. Gordon would make everything seem all right, of course he would, with his dry Scots humour, his ability to exude an air of complete calm, his air of always being in complete control of any situation. That was Gordon in a nutshell—and Kim could not imagine a more unlikely pair than he and Bryce Drovnik. Partners! In what?

There were voices, coming nearer, men's voices —and laughter. And then a pause, and the door opened, and Gordon came in, followed by Bryce. Kim put the cat down and went forward to his open arms.

'Kim, my dear! What a surprise!' He would never lose that soft Highland lilt as long as he lived. It was as much a part of him as the limp which was a permanent reminder of that day seven years ago when he had taken his last climb with John Dalby. And only Gordon had returned. He was like a second father to Kim and she loved him dearly.

'I came instead of Jack. He went haring off to South America the day before your telegram came.

You know Jack.'

'Do I know Jack!' Gordon threw back his head and roared with laughter. 'Do I not? So you came in his place, hmm—' and he turned to Bryce, and the glance they exchanged was full of meaning.

If only he would leave the room! But you couldn't ask your host to do that. And then Bryce spoke:

'You will be hungry, Gordon,' he said. 'I will see if Ann has your meal ready.'

'Thanks, Bryce.' There was a moment's silence when he went out, then Kim spoke. There wasn't much time before he returned.

'Gordon,' she began, 'who *is* he?'

He went over to the chair opposite Kim's and sat down. 'Ah, that's better. Who is Bryce? An old friend—a very good friend.'

'He didn't want me here,' she said.

'No, I know. Och, Kim, it's very difficult, my dear, I just don't know what to say. You know I'm absolutely delighted to see you here and if it were left to me——' he shrugged, and gave her one of his slow smiles.

'Can't you persuade him?' she said. 'You know I'm as good as Jack——'

'Better, my sweet, better—but you know Jack, whatever his faults he has one great gift, that of utter and total discretion—and I'm afraid, when Bryce finds out what your job is——' He stopped, but too late, because the door had opened too silently for them to notice, and Bryce had been standing there. For how long?

'What is Miss Dalby's job, Gordon?' he asked. They both turned—Bryce had never seemed so big or formidable as at that moment. Kim knew a sweeping sensation of apprehension. And something else. A nagging memory, returning again, but not vague now; clearer. Much clearer.

Gordon gave Kim an apologetic grimace as Bryce crossed the room towards them, moving with a panther-like grace that belied his size.

Kim looked up at Bryce. 'I'm a journalist, Mr Drovnik,' she answered. 'I'll save Gordon the embarrassment of telling you. I work freelance, and I travel all over the world in search of a good story—and usually find it. But that isn't why I came here. I came solely to help Gordon out, because I'm due for a break, and I owe him a lot. Is that what you want to know?'

'It is enough.' Bryce might have been angry, it was hard to tell. Dark features, the eyes cooler than before, his mouth unsmiling, only the subtle atmosphere of tension in the room coming across quite strongly to Kim, and undoubtedly to Gordon who looked faintly uneasy. Unusual for Gordon, because he was the calmest person she had ever met, unflappable, urbane. But not at this moment. Kim longed to reassure him, because in a way it was nothing to do with him. Her battle was with Bryce Drovnik. No longer her imagination, the antagonism was there between them like an electric current. She didn't like him, and he didn't like her—she was quite sure of that now.

'I am sorry, Miss Dalby, but I think it better for you to leave here. Not at once, of course. You are welcome to stay over the weekend—and then on Monday I will have Gordon take you to Vienna by helicopter—or I myself will do it.'

'Because you don't want me to know what you are looking for?' Kim asked, and saw Gordon's slight frown, because he knew there was something in the way she was saying it...

'The trouble is, I have a good memory—almost photographic, in fact. As Gordon will tell you. And as we came back from the lake this morning—just after we encountered the two dogs, as a matter of fact—something stirred in the back of my mind. It's been bothering me all day—but it isn't any more. I know what that memory was. Do you want me to tell you?'

You could have cut the atmosphere in that quiet room with a knife.

'I think you had better,' said Bryce softly. Very softly—menacingly. She was almost frightened, but it had gone too far for her to back down now.

'When I started work on a newspaper seven years ago, at the age of sixteen, my job was to make the tea and generally run errands—but I also had the time to read back numbers of papers in their library—and one story fascinated me because, like everyone else, talks of missing treasures are fascinating, however old or young you are. It was only a very small item and I might have missed it altogether if there hadn't been a particularly beautiful picture of a place I'd spent many holidays in as a child—but I did see it, and it stuck in my mind.' She stopped. Both men were listening, Gordon with a kind of resigned patience as if in the face of the inevitable, Bryce with a grim intensity that was daunting. 'It reported that a plane had crashed and been lost somewhere in Austria.' She had to take a deep breath now. 'It—the plane—was rumoured to be carrying a magnificent collection of jewellery that was being taken for safety from the state museum in Budapest to Western Europe only hours before the—the Russians entered the city——' she faltered, because the silence was frightening. 'And that's—all.'

Gordon let out his breath in a heavy sigh of despair. 'Oh, Kim,' he said. 'Oh, *Kim*!'

'I'm sorry, Gordon.' She turned to him. 'But I had to tell you. It's never been found, has it? That's what you're looking for?'

It was Bryce who answered. 'So, you know. And what do you intend to do about it?'

She looked up at him. 'Nothing. What should I do?'

'You are a—journalist.' He made it sound like a dirty word. 'If you go—if you leave here now—there will soon be crowds of people coming to search. Do you think we want that?'

Kim's anger rose swiftly as she stood up to go towards him. 'What do you think I am? Do you imagine I'm going to tell everyone? Gordon is my friend—he was my father's best friend——'

'And you like a good story—I believe those were your own words—do you think I imagine you will go home and say nothing?'

'Yes, I do as a matter of fact!' She longed to strike that dark lean face, if only to wipe the hard scorn from it. Her fingers itched to do so, but she would control herself while Gordon was there.

And Gordon stood too and came behind her, putting his arm round her shoulders. He was just about to speak when the door opened, Matthew came in, and said: 'Mr Hillaby's meal is ready, sir.' If he too noticed any atmosphere his face gave nothing away. He went out, closing the door quietly after him.

Bryce said quietly: 'You had better go and eat, Gordon. I want to talk to Miss Dalby.'

'But——' Gordon looked acutely unhappy, and Kim said softly:

'It's all right. You go.' She smiled at him.

He sighed heavily. 'All right.' He limped out, and Kim felt a sensation of relief. *Now* she could tell Bryce Drovnik exactly what she thought of him. But she didn't get the chance. He closed the door after Gordon, came over to where she stood, and said forcefully:

'So. Gordon is too gentle. I am not. And I will tell you now that I do not trust you or your kind. I never have and I never will, and if you think you are leaving here to go and spread your story you are very much mistaken, Miss Dalby!'

She listened to his words with growing horror. He was actually threatening her! 'Just a moment,' she said. 'Let's get one thing *quite* clear. Are you trying to tell me that you won't *allow* me to leave?'

'You are almost precisely right,' he answered. 'You will not be locked up, or anything like that, but you came here to do some underwater swimming, and that is precisely what you will now stay and do.'

'You can't talk to me like that!' She felt quite breathless.

'But I am doing so. You have offered to take your brother's place. So—now you may do so.'

'There's a difference,' she said slowly, 'between volunteering—and in being *told* what to do.'

'Maybe. But that is the situation. You will stay here.'

'Try and stop me walking out!' she challenged.

He began to smile. 'You talk tough—just as I imagine a journalist might do. One minute you are full of the desire to help your dear friend Gordon, the next, because you do not like my words, you are bristling like an indignant cat. Do you think I would allow someone like you to spoil plans that have been maturing for months? Have no fear, you will be comfortable and well fed here. And you will be helping Gordon. Remember that. He is not a well man. This treasure hunt is as much his idea as mine——'

'That's blackmail!' she protested.

'Yes? You call it that? How amusing. It was precisely what you had in mind when you told us of your good memory, was it not? Are you frightened of me?

The question took her by surprise, but she rallied swiftly. 'Of *you*? Why should I be?'

'You are acting as if I threaten you.'

'You just did, saying you wouldn't let me leave!'

'That was not a threat, Miss Dalby, it was a promise. We are very remote here, our only contact with the outside world by car or helicopter. You could not walk to the station even if you knew the way. It is many kilometres away—you fell asleep, remember?'

'You have a phone,' she said. 'I don't like being told what to do. Especially not by hostile Russians.' She was nearly trembling, but whether with rage or fear, she did not know. She did know that she had never encountered anyone like Bryce Drovnik before, and that in itself was daunting.

'You make it sound like an insult,' he said softly. 'It is very many years ago that I left my native land. I would choose my words more carefully if I were you.' He had gone slightly pale, as if with temper.

'But you're not me, are you?' she retorted swiftly. 'And I'm not someone you can boss about. When I tell Gordon what you've been saying, he won't like it either.'

'You are free to do so. How could I stop you?' But his words had a quality that filled her with doubt. It was as if he knew something she didn't. It was as if he *waited*.

'Why do you say it like that?' she said, after a tension-filled pause.

'I think you know. You have seen Gordon. Tell me, does he not seem different to you?'

'He is—quieter than I remembered,' she admitted at last.

'He is not well, as I said before. He is having treatment for a nervous condition. A legacy of the mountaineering accident seven years ago.'

'My father died in that accident,' she said.

'I know. He told me when he mentioned Jack to me. Gordon tried to save your father's life—perhaps you did not know that. That memory will

35

never leave him—that he failed to do so.'

Kim felt very weary all of a sudden, and weak. It must have shown in her face, for the man's own expression altered—only fractionally, but he said in a voice that was almost gentle: 'Go ahead, tell him. I will not try to stop you. The choice is yours.'

But he had won, and they both knew it. He was hard—as hard as granite. And unfeeling. Or was he? Just for a second she had seen something in those greeny-grey eyes that might have been compassion. Quickly banished, and it might have been her imagination, but it was no longer important.

'I'll stay,' she said.

'Yes, I knew you would. It is not my wish—you know that. But I too have no choice.'

'It is for Gordon, not for *you*.' Her eyes met his and she didn't attempt to hide her contempt.

'I know that too. At least we understand one another, do we not?' He stood there before her, over six feet of muscle and strength, and she thought she had never hated anyone so much in all her life.

CHAPTER THREE

And after all that, Bryce set out to show Kim what a good host he could be. It was almost effortless, she could see that. It didn't alter her feelings towards him one iota, but at least it was better, she reflected later that evening, being a captive in a velvet padded cell instead of a cold dungeon.

There were drinks, and both men smoked cigars after they had all finished eating, and they sat in that beautiful room at the back of the house and talked of the plans for systematically combing every inch of the lake bed. The black cat sat curled up on Kim's knee, purring, half asleep, and she put her head back against the chair and let it all wash over her.

'Are you tired, Kim?' Gordon, his voice concerned, asked her.

She smiled. 'No. I was listening.' But she didn't look at Bryce when she said it. She preferred not to. There was so much she needed to know from Gordon, but not yet, not yet.

And then Bryce said the words that she now realised she had been subconsciously awaiting. 'Miss Dalby and I went into the lake this morning,' he said to Gordon, and he looked at her as he said it.

'Kim,' she said. 'My name is Kim.' His formal use of her name—done deliberately, she felt sure—was annoying.

'Kim—of course. Thank you.' He nodded gravely, as if the idea amused him. 'I trust you will call me Bryce?'

'Is that your real name?' It came out more bluntly than she had intended, and she saw Gordon's slight frown, and wished that she had phrased it more tactfully. But Bryce appeared not to notice.

'It is, let us say, an anglicised version of my correct name, which would be far too difficult for a western tongue to get around. Why, does it bother you?'

'No, of course not.' No doubt about it, she felt

reprimanded.

He turned to Gordon again, and smiled. 'Kim is an excellent swimmer.'

'I taught them both—Jack and Kim. Good pupils they were.'

'I am sure. Tomorrow morning we will go over the lake in the helicopter. Then we can make our plans. It could take weeks, you realise that, M—— Kim?'

'I suppose so.' But she hadn't really.

'Good. Now if you will excuse me, I have some work to do. I'm sure that you both have much to say to each other. Ring for Matthew if you need anything. Goodnight.'

He left them and the room was empty without him.

Gordon let out a long slow sigh. 'Oh dear,' he said.

Kim went over to sit at his feet. 'Oh dear yes,' she echoed. 'Is he always like that?'

He laughed. 'Bryce? I've never seen any two people strike sparks off each other like you two. The room positively bristles with electricity when you're together! Still——' he looked reflective, 'it might not be a bad thing.'

'In what way?' Kim was puzzled, as well as dismayed. Was it so obvious?

'In your underwater search for the plane. There'll be no room for complacency. You'll both be—metaphorically speaking—on your toes.'

She could well imagine that. 'Mmm, yes,' she said. 'Tell me about him. I know he's a Russian. He's obviously wealthy if this house is his. But that's all. Is he married?' She had no idea why she asked that. She had certainly had no intention. But the question had popped out almost without her knowing.

'Married? No! He's like me, a crusty old bachelor—no! That's stupid.' Gordon grinned and ruffled Kim's hair. 'He's not married, but he has plenty of women after him, and he likes their company—generally speaking,' he looked at her and smiled slightly. 'You seem to have rubbed him up the wrong way somewhat, but that will pass.'

'I doubt it,' she said dryly. 'He's the most aggressive man I've ever met.'

'He's not usually.' He shook his head. 'Still, he's had a hard life. He's had to work like a beaver for everything's he's ever made, and I admire him for that, and I daresay you don't make a fortune by being soft.'

'How long have you known him?' Kim persisted.

'Och, about fifteen—twenty years. He was a young man then, but with one outstanding talent. He has a brilliant head for figures—absolutely brilliant. He came on a climb once and told me something about his plans. He even managed to fire me with enthusiasm—and you know me, I can't add two and two together without difficulty.' Kim smiled at the exaggeration, but she knew how unworldly Gordon was. 'He got himself two jobs, one during the day teaching people to ski, the other at night waiting on tables in one of Vienna's most famous hotels. And he saved every penny he earned and then began to play the stock market. We've always kept in touch, one way or another, and then, about three years ago, he decided he'd like a home of his own—something he had literally never known before in his life. In his younger years, when his parents fled Russia, they lived with friends, at hostels, anywhere they could find to lay their heads. All Bryce has ever known is insecurity, which is why I admire him all the more, because in spite of all you have seen of him, and think of him, he is a very well balanced man.'

'Hmm,' said Kim, fascinated by all that Gordon was telling her, but hardly able to agree with that. 'So what made him come here?' she asked.

'It was quite by chance—and I played a part in it, I'm glad to say. We'd bumped into one another in Vienna where I'd been staying, writing a book on mountaineering—and he told me he would like to buy something, and I knew the d'Arcy Browns who lived here and were contemplating selling to go and live in America. I introduced them, and bingo! the next thing I knew there was a call from Bryce telling me he'd bought the place together with resident staff and a couple of gardeners——' so that explained Ann and Matthew. 'And I was welcome to stay any time.' He paused to take a sip of fine old brandy and Kim smiled at him with affection. The sandy hair was thinner now, as was his face, but the stubborn Scots jaw was as firm as ever. 'Go on,' she urged. 'I'm fascinated.'

'I visited him, of course, and then went back to Vienna. Then, a couple of months ago, he turned up on my doorstep with an intriguing story. You can imagine what it was—but there was a curious twist to it. What had happened was this. Everyone had forgotten about this plane that had supposedly crashed in the mountains somewhere in Austria. Search parties had looked for months with no success, and it was assumed that it must have landed in deep snow and been buried for ever. But now here's the twist. When Bryce first moved in, there were two gardeners—brothers, still are—and one day they brought their father with them. He was ancient, very doddery, nearly ninety, and considered by everyone to be completely senile. He couldn't be left alone because both wives had gone to a family funeral near Vienna, so the two sons had, very apologetically, brought the old man up here and sat him on a seat and told him not to move while they got on with their gardening. To cut a long story short, Bryce had told them to bring him into the house—it was an icy cold day—and had got talking to him. Poor old fellow, no one ever talked or listened to him. He must have thought it was his birthday to have someone actually interested in what he had to say. He has a great compassion for old people, has Bryce.

'Where was I? Oh yes, quite simply, the old man told him about the huge flying saucer that he'd seen land in the Schwartzee—that lake—one night years ago when he was looking for lost sheep. Only trouble is, as he confided to Bryce, no one believed him when he got around to telling them because he was actually slightly the worse for drink anyway and had been seeing things for years. That was all. The old man went, and although Bryce was tempted to dismiss it also, something made him go to a map and check up. What he found there sent him flying to Vienna to see me—and after I'd had a look, and done some quiet checking up myself on old newspaper files to see the plane's intended destination, I began to get that tingle that tells you you're on to something. Allowing for slight pilot error—and there was a snowstorm over these hills the night of the crash—this lake is in a direct line with his ultimate destination. And the reason that the plane has never been found is because it's buried under sixty feet of water somewhere in the Schwartzee.'

Kim held her breath. The picture Gordon had painted was an intriguing one—but already her journalistic brain was racing ahead, checking, assessing probabilities and improbabilities. Then she let her breath out slowly. 'But Gordon,' she said at last. 'Didn't he—Bryce—check up on *when* exactly the old man had seen his "flying saucer"? That would simplify matters enormously.'

'Yes, true. He tried. He went down to visit the old fellow a few days later, taking some soup from Ann that he had particularly enjoyed the day he was here, but he could get no sense out of him at all. And as it was still just an idea, he didn't want anyone else to know—for obvious reasons—but the old fellow had completely forgotten everything they had spoken about. And a few weeks later he died. And that was that. But by this time we were both so fired with the idea that Bryce sent for me again—said to bring my typewriter and do my writing here in peace, an offer I jumped at as my apartment in Vienna is pretty noisy. He knew of my underwater activity years ago, and wanted my ad-

42

vice and help in planning an underwater search. And we've done some business deals together—I've managed to help him make contacts—that sort of stuff—so here I am.'

'And that's when you decided to send for Jack.'

'After we had talked it over and I'd told him some of Jack's adventures. Yes.'

'Hm. And you got me.'

Gordon laughed. 'Yes.' Then he sobered. 'You can't do this kind of thing alone. There has to be at least two. On the other hand, the less anyone knows, the better. This is why Bryce resents you, I'm afraid, because you're a journalist.'

'No.' Kim shook her head firmly. 'He didn't know my job when I arrived. The simple fact that I was a *woman* was what put *him* off, I can tell you. Is he a woman-hater?'

A wry smile. 'Hardly,' said Gordon dryly. 'But you must admit it's a bit of a shock to find yourself confronted by a female scuba diver when you're expecting a man.'

'It wasn't just that,' Kim insisted. 'He got my back up straight away with his arrogance. A sort of "well, you'll be no good, so you can go home" kind of attitude.'

'Are you sure you're not being too sensitive?' Gordon asked gently. 'After all, in your job you must come across a certain amount of male prejudice——'

'Precisely,' said Kim crisply, 'so I can spot it a mile off.'

Gordon couldn't hide a grin. 'Is that why you took such delight in telling him about your good memory for old newspaper stories?'

'Yes,' admitted Kim. She shivered. 'Brrr, I could feel the icicles forming as I spoke! Was he very angry?'

'I've never seen him in a temper—but yes, I'd say he wasn't very pleased. And what *did* he say when I'd gone? I hated to leave you—but I sensed that he wanted to talk privately.' So now they had reached the moment of truth. The moment when, if she told Gordon what Bryce had *really* said, he would be angry and upset. And would insist on her being free to leave if she chose.

'Why, not much,' she smiled. 'Merely that he would appreciate me keeping quiet—that he would trust me to do so, as you had assured him, and that I could stay and work with him.'

Gordon was looking at her in a very old-fashioned way. 'Hmphm,' he said at last. 'I *see*. So everything's all right, is it?'

Kim gave him a sunny smile. 'Inasmuch as it ever will be with the two of us—yes.'

'Well, that's good enough. I know how capable you are. I should do, I taught you. And you'll learn to get along better.'

Kim doubted that very much. But at least he believed her. That was the important thing. 'We can always hope for a miracle,' she said warmly, and saw Gordon's face crease into a smile.

'Och, you're a bonny wee girl, my Kim,' he said. 'But you're an obstinate creature as well. Just remember, though—so is Bryce. Don't go banging your head on a brick wall with him. I'm afraid you'd be hurt if you did. And I like you both too

44

much to have to referee any battles.'

'Battles? Really, Gordon!' Kim laughed. 'You're reading too many books. Don't *worry*.' She reached up and hugged him impulsively. 'I shall be a perfect lady.'

He looked faintly alarmed. 'That would be rather a strain,' he said impishly. 'Just be yourself—I prefer that—but just remember, he's not an ordinary man. You'll never twist him round your little finger like you do most of the fellows you've known——'

'I don't know what you mean,' she said demurely.

'Och, you do fine well! I've seen you bat those long eyelashes many times. But remember, with him, it's a working partnership, and you'll get on splendidly.'

Will we? thought Kim. I wonder?

Sunday was another crisp early autumn day, and after breakfast, Bryce said to Kim: 'Are you ready to come up in the helicopter and have a look at the lake with me?'

'Ready when you are.' She put down her empty coffee cup and stood up. 'I'll just go and get my coat, if you'll excuse me.' She managed to wink at Gordon, unseen by Bryce, as she went out, and heard his muffled snort. All through breakfast she had been sweetness itself—not too obviously so— just enough, and Bryce had responded by being coolly courteous, an ideal host in fact. And Gordon had watched, and you could tell, thought Kim, that he wondered at it—knowing Kim as he did, and presumably Bryce as well.

Bryce stood up when she entered the dining room again. She was dressed in her warm check coat with its furry black collar and hood.

'I'm ready,' she said softly, and smiled at them both, waiting, meekly it seemed, for instruction.

'Then we will go.' He opened the door again for her to precede him.

'Good luck,' Gordon called, and she smiled inwardly. Perhaps the words were not as simple as they seemed.

Bryce led the way out of the back of the house to where the helicopter waited, a huge silent machine, on its concrete strip. 'You have been in one before?' he asked her as he swung the door open and gave her his arm to help her up.

'Yes, several times.' But she wasn't going to tell him when. Gordon wasn't there any more. There was no need to pretend. And Bryce sensed it too, she knew that with a sure intuition. The atmosphere, the clear cold air of that day, was spiced with the tension that existed between them, and when they were both seated inside, and the door was closed, Bryce turned to her.

'So,' he said quietly. 'You did not tell Gordon?'

'Of course not. You didn't expect me to, did you?'

'No. So now we understand each other.'

'Only too well. He has a high opinion of you. I can't imagine he would take the thought of you threatening me with equanimity.'

Bryce's mouth twisted in a smile that lacked humour. 'No, that is true,' he admitted. 'So now we

46

are partners—and from now on, in the water, you will do as I tell you.'

'I didn't expect you'd put *me* in charge of the expedition,' she answered dryly. 'Don't worry, I'll do as I'm told. It is your idea, after all.'

'Gordon told you the story?'

'Yes.'

'Good. That will save me doing so. Do you believe it is feasible that the plane is here somewhere?'

'Are you interested in my opinion?'

He gave her a level sideways glance. 'In this matter, yes.' It warned her.

'Then I think it's very possible. Yes,' she answered. But that look of his had stung her. Who did he think he was? 'Although I can't imagine why you need to find treasure. Haven't you enough?'

'I have my reasons—and they are nothing to do with you. Do not fear, Kim, you will be paid for your time here——'

'I didn't mean *that*!' she burst out, dismayed. In an odd way, he always managed to twist whatever she said round, and then come out with a devastatingly cutting remark. 'I meant——'

'Please do not trouble yourself to argue. We will get along far better if we both refrain from personal remarks, I think. Do you not agree?'

She held her temper in with difficulty. The arrogance—the sheer *arrogance* of the man!

'As you are the boss,' she answered, 'I have no choice but to agree with you, have I?'

'I have never expected anyone to accede to my

47

wishes without argument—or to put it more simply, I do not like "yes-men" I believe the expression is—or in your case "yes-women"—so let us get that quite straight immediately.' It was said without humour, without in fact, much expression at all, but it was there all right, the hard, implacable strength that told her more than the words could.

She shivered, unable to help herself, and he looked at her coolly. 'Perhaps we had better go.' He leaned forward to the controls and the powerful rotor blades whirred into life above them.

There was that incredible moment of lift off when you felt as if you were going to leave your stomach behind. Then, as it passed, Kim looked out of the windows and marvelled at the sheer beauty of their surroundings. Suddenly all petty dislikes and squabbles seemed so very unimportant beside the majestic grandeur of towering mountains, so insignificant.

'What a lovely place,' she whispered, uncaring if he heard or not. The engines were loud, and perhaps he didn't and he was concentrating anyway, dark face intent on the controls, his hands firmly on the joystick. Kim turned away again from him, because there was something very disturbing about those dark features, and she didn't understand why she found it so—which was in itself disturbing.

Soaring to the right of them was the Weissberg— White Mountain—the one of that last fateful climb of Gordon and her father, seven years previously. And somewhere near here he was buried, in a little churchyard that had seen many such tragedies. Tears sprang to Kim's eyes at the memories of so long ago. While she was here she would go up there and see the grave. Gordon would take her. Dear Gordon! Anything she did would be for him, not for the unsmiling stranger by her side. And that made her feel better.

A touch on her arm; she turned, blinking away the last remains of tears. Bryce was pointing, and shouting something which was unintelligible above the roar of the engines, but she guessed what he was trying to say, and nodded.

They had circled the lake, so that a vast expanse stretched before them, and at the far end was his house, gleaming whitely in a watery sun. Kim caught her breath at the cool beauty of it all. Bryce was going down, and he put binoculars in her hands and Kim scanned the dark waters of the lake. White Mountain—Black Lake. Strange contrast of names. The black unruffled surface hid its secrets well. Only a bird, skimming low across its face, causing faint ripples, disturbed it. There was something faintly sinister about it, for all its beauty, and she shivered slightly.

Lower, lower, and lower still they skimmed, like that bird, and Kim had the strange sensation that they were going to dive down, and down ... And now she could almost reach out and touch the lake, and she felt frightened, panicking suddenly and quite illogically, so much so that she leaned over to touch Bryce's arm, and he, seeing her expression, lifted the helicopter so that they soared upwards again.

He was watching her, dark, puzzled. He picked up his headphones and pointed for her to do the same, which she did.

His voice was suddenly too close. 'What is the matter?' he said, into her ear. The mouthpiece was inches away from her face. She whispered:

'I thought we were going into the water,' feeling slightly ashamed. She thought the corner of his mouth twitched, but it could have been imagination.

'There is no danger. This machine cost too much for me to do that. I was letting you see how daunting is our task, that was all. When we return I will show you a detailed chart of the lake, and how we will plan our dives to cover certain areas. Have you seen enough? Do you wish to return?'

'Yes.' Then, quickly, on impulse, 'No. May we see the—the White Mountain?'

'If you wish.' But the look he gave her was odd. He knew, of course. They soared away from the lake, their shadow diminishing as they rose, and headed towards the grim white peaks of the mountain range. There was only one she watched, intently, as they neared it, sadly, feeling the old aching hurt that returned occasionally.

The grass of the fields and lower reaches were left behind them as they climbed, and she saw the cruel jagged rocks and ice patches, the eternal snow, higher still the glacier-like surface that had challenged men over the years—and claimed its victims.

Kim sighed. And the sensitive microphone must have picked up the sigh, for Bryce said: 'You have seen enough?'

'Yes.' Her eyes travelled away from the stark

reality of the mountain, further down in the valley she saw the little white church and knew it was the one. People were walking towards it, little knots of two or three, brightly clad figures as small as children from that distance. Of course, it was Sunday. She even imagined she could hear the bells above the noise of the rotors. He was there, somewhere, her father. Soon she would go and see his grave. Would he approve of what she was doing? Somehow she knew he would. The thought was a comforting one.

The silence was almost deafening. The click-click died away, the helicopter settled, and Bryce turned to her, removing his earphones.

Nothing remained of the tears. Kim looked at him, her normal self again. 'We'll go in and see the chart of the lake now, shall we?' she said brightly.

'Yes, of course.' But he watched her. She looked back at him. He didn't know—he couldn't know—that she had just reached a private decision. She made sure nothing of it showed in her face for him to see. It didn't concern him anyway. But he would find out soon enough when they began diving. He would discover just how good she was, and he would be surprised. And she gave a little smile. Easing himself out of his seat, he scrambled down to the ground and waited for her.

For a moment she was in his arms. Just for a second, as she jumped down, but her whole body tingled at his touch, at an awareness of his strength as he had effortlessly lifted her down. Then the spell was broken as the two alsatians bounded up, no longer wary of Kim, and Gordon appeared at the door and waved. Kim turned and walked away from Bryce. She didn't want him to see her face. Not just now—not yet.

'Hello, Kim. Enjoy your little ride?'

'Mmm, yes, it was lovely.' She linked her arm in his and Bryce came up behind them and said:

'I hope you've ordered coffee?'

'I have,' Gordon laughed. 'Ann's doing it now.'

'Good. We have a busy morning ahead of us. We are going to plan the search.' Bryce spoke calmly, coolly, logically. And suddenly Kim knew what Gordon had meant when he had been speaking about Bryce the previous evening. This man would succeed in whatever he set out to do. There was nothing brash or reckless in his manner, but instead a hard decisiveness, a certainty of his own capabilities. And now it seemed even more important for her not to let her father—or Gordon— down.

Kim put her hand to her aching head. How long before they could eat lunch? Her mind was a whirl of figures and diagrams as she sat at a large table with the two men, and listened, and added her opinions—and watched Bryce as he put his points across.

'Had enough?' Gordon's voice was full of understanding, and Bryce looked up at that so that their eyes met in a cool silent clash.

'I think we will stop now. Kim looks tired.' No sympathy there—nothing.

'I'm not,' she denied.

'It does not matter.' He was already folding the

map carefully. 'We can return to it after we have eaten. I will see Ann.'

He went out and Kim looked at Gordon. 'Don't give him the chance,' she begged. Gordon knew what she meant and grinned.

'He's all right,' he said. 'But he does tend to lose count of time when he's engrossed in something.'

'I know,' said Kim. 'Only then he gave me that "she's a feeble woman" look—he's so damned *patronising*!'

'You'll get used to it,' Gordon laughed. 'I thought you were made of tougher material.'

'I'm learning fast, believe me. I hope he doesn't expect me to swim to the point of exhaustion every day. There is a limit.'

'Don't worry, he won't. You need to be fresh for that sort of work—and he knows that as well as anyone. I think the way we've planned it is very practical actually. A definite area each day. My only regret is that I can't join you. Still, I'll be in the boat with cameras and torches and everything you need. It'll go well, have no doubt.'

'I wonder if we'll find the plane?' asked Kim.

Gordon looked at her. 'I wonder,' he said softly. 'We'll see, won't we?'

CHAPTER FOUR

THEY were to begin the following morning at nine, dive for two hours, stop and eat, and then go down again early afternoon. And that would be the pattern of their days until the search succeeded. And now we know, thought Kim. It was mid-afternoon on Sunday. The chart had been folded away for the second time, and Bryce turned and said to Kim and Gordon: 'Shall we go for a ride?'

'Lovely!' Gordon stood up and stretched. 'Just what I need. Kim?'

'Yes, please.' She wondered why he had asked. Gordon went out, presumably for his coat, and the two of them were left on their own.

'Well?' asked Bryce.

'Well what?' She said it calmly enough, she thought.

'You find the arrangements satisfactory? You said little.'

'There was no need. You are so completely in charge,' she answered dryly.

'Ah yes? Good. That is as it should be, no? But you are still entitled to say if something does not suit you, you know.'

'Why, thank you!' She opened her eyes wide and looked at him. 'I must remember that.' She didn't trouble to hide the sarcasm, and saw his crooked grin. Perhaps he possessed a sense of humour after all.

'Tell me,' he said softly, 'are all English girls like

you?'

'I don't know,' she retorted. 'What am I like?'

'Intelligent, determined to have your own way—sure of yourself——'

'Is that how I strike you?' she asked. 'How strange. Because that's just what I was thinking about *you*. Perhaps it has nothing to do with nationality or sex after all. It must be our personalities. They say that similar types never get on well,' and she gave him a sweet smile and stood up, ready to go out. 'Excuse me, I'll fetch my coat.' But as she moved away, Bryce caught her arm, not ungently.

'Wait a moment. What do you mean?'

She looked down at where his hand rested on her forearm. 'Take your hand away,' she said.

He did so, slowly. 'You do not like being touched?' he was almost amused.

'By you, no. It's not part of the contract, is it?' Then, as he stood, still unmoving, before her, 'Or is it? Perhaps that is something we had better get clear.' Their eyes met, and the tension was there again, filling the room, almost stifling.

His eyes narrowed, a muscle moved in his cheek, and he said softly: 'Explain yourself, please.'

'I shouldn't need to. But if you want me to, I will. I'll spell it out good and clear. I'm here to help you look for a plane, and that's all. A purely business arrangement, as you have been at pains to tell me. And impersonal.' And she smiled slowly at him because she had flicked him on the raw and the expression on his face gave her a slight feeling of satisfaction for all the things he had said to her.

'You are a guest in my house.' He spoke slowly and clearly, and his eyes had gone hard and cold. 'You insult me.'

'Do I really?' She would not let him frighten her, even though the hardness of his eyes was daunting. 'But I'm more of a prisoner than a guest, I thought. You can hardly insult a gaoler, I imagine.' She heard him draw in his breath sharply, and knew she had gone too far.

He seemed to speak with an effort. 'I think you had better go and get your coat,' he grated, 'before I say something I will regret.' And he stood aside to let her pass.

The atmosphere was electric, as if it might explode at any moment. He stood there, large, powerful—dignified—and filled with anger. Kim found the strength to move and went quickly past him and out of the door. Gordon was returning, but she could not have spoken had she tried. She moved past him, wordless, and knew he was staring after her, and that on his face would be puzzlement, but she could help it.

Safely in her room she put her hands to her burning cheeks. What on earth had induced her to speak as she had? She didn't know. Perhaps she never would. She just didn't understand why this dark Russian could have such a terrible effect on her. And of one thing she was quite sure. As she moved across to her wardrobe for her coat, she knew with dread certainty that Bryce Drovnik would neither forgive nor forget her remarks. There was one thing she could not know: what, if anything, he might do about it.

The incident might never have been. On the way from the house, in the sleek Mercedes, Bryce was once more the considerate host. Gordon sat beside him at the front, Kim behind Gordon so that all she saw of her host was a hard profile. It was tempting to watch him, for she could do so quite unobserved. Why she should want to, she didn't know. She didn't like him, she certainly didn't find him attractive, although she had to admit there was undoubtedly an air about him that women could find intriguing. It's my journalistic mind, she decided —simply curiosity at what makes him tick. And she smiled to herself a little at having found a logical reason for her desire to stare at him. He probably would make a good story, she thought. A profile of a man who had climbed from obscurity to fortune simply by hard work—and something else. Not luck, although that was always an element: personality. That was it. Kim could picture him as he had been, teaching middle-aged matrons to ski— waiting on tables in a restaurant, never putting a foot wrong so that he would inevitably be well liked. Saving all he could, shrewdly assessing the market—perhaps even overhearing information at table or on the slopes that would help him.

She could see it as clearly as if it were already written down. And as she did so, the idea came to her—the idea of actually doing such a story herself. She could imagine his reaction if she asked him bluntly—and smiled to herself. How much better to think about it secretly, listen to all Gordon had to say—make private notes, compose it into some kind of order on paper—and then when it was done, ask him to look at it—see his reaction. There would be time while she was here. It would not all be work, she knew that already. There would be much private time when she could let her mind roam at will over the composition of a brief life story of a very interesting personality. The tingle was in her blood. The flair she possessed that told her when something newsworthy was about to happen was working at full speed. And Kim knew that, come what may, she could—and would—do it. It would, she reasoned to herself, be good practice in writing if nothing else. But even as she thought it, she knew it was more, much more.

She relaxed against the comfortable seat at the back of the car and began to take an interest in her surroundings. They were speeding down a narrow road, well away from the house now, but whether in the direction of the station at which she had first encountered Bryce, she could not tell. The sky was darker as evening approached, and heavy clouds threatened snow, but nothing could detract from the grave magnificence of the towering mountains surrounding them. Grassy fields stretched away on either side of their route, bright green, dotted with blue flowers—so soon to be covered with snow, when winter came. Trees grew in profusion, far away a tall forest on the lower slopes of a mountain added a dark contrast to the whiteness of ice and snow, and Kim's heart ached because this was the land her father had loved—and died in.

The men were talking, not excluding her deliberately she knew, but discussing business, and she began to listen because it was all grist to the mill, and might help her to understand the way his mind worked. Gordon had mentioned that they were partners and it seemed probable that it was in more than just the treasure hunt, for their talk ranged over a variety of things that she would normally have found uninteresting, but didn't now. Gordon had no head for figures, she knew, but he was deeply intelligent in other ways, and had that particular gift of making friends wherever he went. Names were mentioned casually; people whose names appeared in the newspapers from time to time in connection with all kinds of enterprises, and whose wealth was a byword. It was not deliberate name-dropping—it was quite simply that Bryce and Gordon lived in a different world.

Kim's fingers itched to make notes. Her reporter's pad was in her bag—she never went anywhere without it, and her shorthand was excellent. But the time for any jottings would be when she was alone, she knew that.

The car was slowing down, stopping. Kim, aware that she had not been concentrating on the ride, because of her own inner thoughts, sat up and looked to see why. They were on a stretch of comparatively straight road, and there was no other traffic, as there had not been for a while, none moving, at any rate. The reason for Bryce's halt was apparent immediately, for a long American car was standing at the side of the road, and a man and woman were looking into the open bonnet, clearly dismayed.

Then they looked up and waved, and Bryce opened his door and went across to them. It was obvious immediately that they were friends. Even as Gordon turned to Kim and said: 'A couple from near the village—Americans, as you might have guessed from that disgusting vehicle of theirs. Stinking rich from oil—but he doesn't know the back wheel from the front.'

Kim laughed, but she was watching Bryce, tall dark immaculate Bryce who was taking his jacket off, handing it to the man, bending over, fiddling in the engine. She was fascinated, and perhaps something showed in her face, for Gordon smiled and said softly: 'He knows what he's doing. I forgot to tell you he worked in a garage for a while when he first came to Austria.'

'Doesn't he mind getting dirty?' Kim asked. 'I mean, his clothes—that sweater he's wearing, it's cashmere, must have cost a fortune——'

'He won't, you'll see.'

If only she could make some notes now, while it was fresh in her mind. She couldn't, but the next best thing was to observe—and remember the pictures and fix it in her memory for the writing later.

She saw him straighten up, saw the blonde woman hand him a cloth, saw too the smiles on their faces, the words and laughter, then Bryce's nod, his salute of acknowledgement—and then he was striding back to the Mercedes, jacketed again—and immaculate. Gordon turned to Kim. 'See?' he teased her.

'Yes.'

'They want us to have a drink with them at Leo's. I said I would ask you both,' but Bryce was looking at Gordon as he said it, and Kim knew that in an odd way they were not remotely concerned in her opinion.

'It might be better to get it over with now—and they are the best ones to spread the word——'

'That is precisely what I meant,' agreed Bryce in dry tones. And Gordon laughed.

'Then we have about fifteen minutes to get the story straight.'

'Yes,' and Bryce gave the other couple the thumbs up. A long blast of the horn on the other car showed that they had received the signal, then it began to move away.

Bryce turned briefly to Kim before he too started the car. 'We are going on a short visit with that couple,' he said. 'They are the biggest gossips in Austria. If they had the slightest inkling of why you are really here it would be all over the country within hours. So——' and he spared Gordon a brief grin, 'now is the time to put our heads together and agree on a good story.'

A good story, echoed Kim silently. How appropriate—for her. 'Surely I could just be coming to visit Gordon,' she suggested. 'After all, we are old friends.'

Bryce didn't look round from driving. He was keeping a good distance from the other vehicle, almost as if to make sure that they couldn't lip-read anything.

Gordon shook his head. 'Not good enough. They'd want to know *why*, and *how*, and what for.' He was silent for a moment, then turned, grinning broadly. 'Besides, Bryce would hardly entertain *my* old friends, when I'm only supposed to be visiting myself. No, I have a much simpler solution—you can be Bryce's fiancée!'

'What!' Kim nearly choked, and heard Bryce's deep laugh.

'Gordon! What a brilliant idea! It could get Leo's wife off my——' he stopped abruptly. Too abruptly. But Kim, too agitated at Gordon's *preposterous*, outrageous suggestion, didn't notice that —until later on, when she was to remember it.

'Just a moment,' she said very firmly. 'That is ridiculous! How can I——'

'Och, come on now!' remonstrated Gordon. 'Where's your sense of fun? You can do it better than anyone.' And he turned and gave her a look she knew of old, his eyes alight with an honest mischief she had not seen for too long. 'It's only for a wee while, an hour or so, and Bryce and I will be by your side to parry any awkward questions—why, girl, it'll be a hoot!'

'Unless Kim finds the idea too repulsive?' suggested Bryce coolly. She let out her breath in a long quiet sigh. The memory of their last, explosive scene, just before the ride, was only too painfully clear. He could not have planned his revenge—for no one could know that a car would break down— but it was ironic that it should have happened. Perhaps, in a way, she owed it to him to accept.

'All right,' she said slowly. 'But what if anyone asks me where—and when—we met?'

Gordon might not have a head for figures, reflected Kim, but he had a fantastically fast brain when it came to making up a quick potted biography. Ten minutes later she had it off pat—and so had Bryce. By the time they arrived at a superb house on the outskirts of a large colourful village, she felt as if she could deal with the most probing questions from anyone.

The American couple were Pearl and Elmer Hailey. Their prospective hosts, Leo and Jeanne Wolfe, were French, and there would be others there too—neither man knew how many. As they walked from the Mercedes towards Pearl and Elmer, Kim said very quietly to Bryce, so that Gordon, slightly ahead of them could not hear: 'I would have dressed and made up with the greatest care had I known I was to be engaged to *you*.'

He looked down at her, a pleasant smile on his face because although not in earshot of the waiting couple, they could be seen very clearly. 'Don't worry,' he said. 'You'll do—*darling*.' The smile was crooked, the last word filled with dark irony—and Kim began to wonder if she was about to make the biggest mistake of her life. How on earth, she thought, a wild inward panic filling her, can you act as though you love a man you heartily detest?

CHAPTER FIVE

BRYCE had sadism perfected to a fine art, reflected Kim as she stood watching him a short while later. He was deriving a cool satisfaction from the situation in which they all now found themselves.

There were twenty or thirty more people in the magnificent salon in which they were drinking. A superbly furnished room, with a roaring log fire, and brilliant chandeliers overhead winking and gleaming their lights on the company. Kim sighed gently and lifted her glass to her lips. She had been to many cocktail parties, tasted many drinks, eaten many of the kind of snacks to be found at such gatherings—but she had never in her life held such an exquisite goblet in her hand: heavy lead-cut crystal, with a rainbow in each facet, it was a pleasure to hold. The wine was sweet and heady—and she knew she had to keep a clear head, now above all else. There must be no slip-ups—for Gordon's sake, not Bryce's.

Jeanne Wolfe was watching her. Kim looked up from her wine and met a cool appraising glance—and remembered something that Bryce had said in the car. What had his words been? 'It could get Leo's wife off my——' He had stopped then, very suddenly. Off my back? That was the obvious conclusion, and Kim wondered, cynically, why. For Jeanne Wolfe was a beautiful woman, dark slumbrous eyes, voluptuous figure, rich deep auburn hair that she wore loose—and a hard look in those eyes as they met Kim's—an expression that she didn't bother to hide. Kim read it quite clearly; no words were needed for a message like that. It was simply: 'What does Bryce see in you?'

Kim smiled slowly and rose to the challenge. 'Madame Wolfe—' what an appropriate name for you, she thought, 'it's so very kind of you to have us here today. We had no idea—' she shrugged grace-

y and looked down at the neat blue trouser suit
wore, 'I would have changed had I known.'

My name is Jeanne,' the other answered. There
a gleam in the dark sultry eyes now. Both knew
re was a little game being played. And she
sn't know the half of it, thought Kim, all *she's*
cerned about is her precious Bryce. If I were
lly engaged to him I would be worried. As it is,
almost priceless.

Thank you—Jeanne. You have a beautiful
se.'

So has Bryce. You will live there after you are
rried?' She had a husky voice, and she looked
nd briefly as she spoke, as if searching for him.
think so.' This could get tricky. Where was
And then she saw him. Both he and Gordon
promised to keep near, but both had been col-
d almost simultaneously by different couples,
ch had resulted in Kim being alone. But he had
ched her—amused—all the time, and now, she
ught, he's coming across to make sure I don't
my foot in it. So here goes, she added to herself,
enjoying himself, let's see what he makes of
. She lifted her arm as he approached.

Hello, darling,' she took his hand and squeezed
resisting the temptation to dig her nails in.
nne was just asking me if we would be living at
house when we're married.'

ryce turned on Kim a look of melting solici-
e. 'We will live wherever you wish to, my dear-
he smiled gently at Jeanne. 'I can refuse her
hing.'

My God! thought Kim. The man is a superb

actor! She saw the almost visible tightening
Jeanne's facial muscles. But the husky voice was
gentle as ever as she said: 'You are such a da
horse, my dear Bryce. Not one of us had any id
you were contemplating marriage until today. Y
could have knocked me down with a feather.'

Yes, you looked as though someone had hit yo
mused Kim, watching the other's face. 'That is t
way I am,' Bryce smiled softly, and looked at Ki
with warmth. 'But I intended giving a party to i
troduce you all, now that Kim is at last here. Ho
ever,' he shrugged gracefully, 'as we have co
here today instead——' he wasn't allowed to fini

'A party? How superb!' Jeanne exclaimed, a
turned. 'Bryce is giving a party for Kim——
Bryce's grip tightened on Kim's—and she realis
with a sense of shock that they were still holdi
hands, and had been doing so for several minut
And she also heard his almost silent oath.

Jeanne had done it so neatly that it *must* ha
been unintentional. Or was it? Judging from t
fleeting expression on Bryce's face, quickly ba
ished, he thought differently. And there was no
ing he could do about it, for glasses were bei
raised in laughing toasts, people were drifting ov
and then they were surrounded by a small crowd
Jeanne and Leo's guests. Pearl Hailey put h
heavily ringed fingers on Kim's arm.

'How lovely!' she drawled. 'And to think we
responsible for bringing you here to Jeanne
dear, all of you, you must all come r to us i
few days. We'll give a little party for Kim first
fore Bryce's.' She beamed on them both, false e

lashes slightly askew, and Kim thought: What on earth have I got myself into? These aren't my kind of people. They may be Bryce's—but they're certainly not mine. And she wished she was anywhere but there.

The ordeal lasted another hour, during which time Kim met Leo, Jeanne's husband, a short fat roly-poly of a man with a ginger wig and clammy hands. He was clearly many years older than his wife, and completely lacking in any sort of charm. She met all the others at the party, and knew she was being weighed up, subtly and expertly. Everyone was extremely friendly and kind on the surface, but she sensed the undercurrents, and was uneasy. Bryce and Gordon rose magnificently to the occasion, virtually answering all question in an easy bantering manner for her. Kim was relieved, for her head had begun to ache with the drink, the smoky atmosphere, the warmth—the sheer strain of pretending to be something she was not.

And then, at last, it was over. The few who were staying for dinner made their farewells to the others who were leaving, and Kim, Bryce, and Gordon walked to the Mercedes after thanking Jeanne and Leo. Kim sank back into her seat, head spinning gently because she had drunk more than she intended, and not eaten enough to counteract the effect.

The headlights searched the drive as they swung round, the last car to do so, and drove off towards the gates. And Gordon let out his breath in a long explosive sigh that said it all for the three of them.

'I wonder what we've let ourselves in for,' he said at last. A huge moon hung low in a clear dark sky, and distant mountain peaks gleamed whitely in its reflected light.

Kim saw Bryce's smile flash briefly as he turned slightly sideways. 'I think,' he said in his deep voice, 'that we all did very well.' Kim watched the hard profile. He was driving in a perfectly relaxed manner—the man in command of the situation. He's enjoying it, she thought, he's actually *enjoying* it. Didn't he care? Didn't he mind that they had all embarked on a series of lies and deception? Apparently not. No wonder he had amassed a fortune from using his wits. He was, she thought, like a computer, not really human at all. But there was one thing that was vaguely disturbing, and it came back at that moment as she regarded him. The touch of his hand had been anything but computer-like. A strong large hand, holding her own as unselfconsciously as if they belonged together, there had been nothing inhuman about that. Her own fingers tingled at the memory, and her face felt so warm that she was thankful for the friendly darkness. More than ever she knew that if she could get all the facets of his disturbing, puzzling personality on to paper, she would have some story.

'And you, Kim, how did you find everybody, hey? Were they not to your liking?' He didn't turn round as he spoke, for all his concentration was on the winding ribbon of road ahead, but she sensed a depth to his question that she didn't understand.

'Do you want a truthful answer, or a polite one?' she asked, and heard Gordon's dry chuckle.

68

'Why, the truth, of course. Do not be afraid that you will offend *me*.' It was there all right, a subtle reminder of their unfortunate scene before leaving his house.

'They're not really my kind of people at all,' she answered slowly, wishing her head was a little clearer, 'so it's hard to say.' Playing for time.

'Then what are your kind of people?' he asked mildly.

'Why, Gordon, for one,' she answered lightly. 'What else?'

And even Bryce joined in the laughter at that. She lay back and closed her eyes, suddenly weary of it all, wishing fervently that Jack hadn't gone chasing off to South America on some ridiculous expedition—then she wouldn't have been in this morass now. And she wouldn't have met Bryce. And that would have been better all round.

'You do realise, don't you,' said Gordon, 'that we are now landed with a party at Pearl's—and one at the house?'

'I regret that,' answered Bryce, looking almost for a moment as if he actually did. 'Jeanne was too quick for me——'

'And she did it deliberately,' interrupted Kim, not sure why she should do so.

'Yes, I know. I did not realise it was so obvious, though.'

'Oh, it wasn't,' she answered sweetly. 'In fact, I didn't think *you'd* notice. Men usually don't. She didn't like me at all.'

Gordon turned round in faint alarm. 'Was she rude to you?'

Kim laughed. 'She was utterly charming—oh, Gordon, you men are so innocent! Two women can have a perfectly normal conversation on the surface, and in actual fact they can be tearing each other to shreds—and only the other women there will know anything is amiss. So I'd prefer to keep out of her way, if you don't mind, because she's going to ask me all sorts of probing questions for a start—and for the second reason, she made it quite clear that she didn't know why on earth Bryce and I should be engaged, and if she continues to get up my nose like that I may be tempted to tell her a few facts of life.' And then, overwhelmed by the force of her outburst, Kim sat back and put a hand to her now aching head. What on earth had possessed her?

There was a strange muffled sound and she opened her eyes in alarm and saw that Gordon was shaking with laughter and searching for a handkerchief.

'Och, deary me!' he managed at last. 'That did me good.' He turned and looked at Kim, and he was still trembling with the aftermath of laughter. 'What a girl you are!'

'I'm glad you think so,' she answered. 'Just as long as you know the situation. I really wouldn't like to let *you* down.' She emphasised the 'you'.

Bryce had remained silent, and she saw that they were nearing his house, and she decided, thankfully, that he really hadn't been listening. She was wrong.

She found out just how wrong she was when they

were back home. It was after dinner, Gordon and Bryce were watching television, and Kim had asked him if she could go and find a book to read from his library.

Peacefully browsing there among the travel books, she looked up when the door opened and Bryce walked in. She knew she should not have been remotely surprised. There had been an awareness in the atmosphere ever since their return, a building up of tension that made her faintly uneasy, and now she sensed that he had come to talk privately to her.

'There are enough books for you?' he asked.

'Yes. Are they your choice, or did they come with the house?' she asked, realising that she could have phrased it more tactfully even as she said it.

He smiled slightly. 'Both. But we do not really want to talk about books, do we?'

'Don't we? You started it.'

He came over to her, and she wished he wouldn't. Somehow it became difficult to think when he was too close, although she could never be sure why that was so. 'I think we understand one another well enough to dispense with the formalities of polite conversation. You know why I am here?'

'I think so. Is it to do with what I said in the car coming back from your friends?'

'It is.' His eyes were darker, deep set and shadowed in the light, and faint shadows emphasised his high cheekbones and stubborn chin. He was a formidable man, she thought. It was the only way to describe him. 'Did you mean what you said?'

'I'm not sure what about. Do you mean about Jeanne not liking me? If so—yes, I did. It was quite obvious—and as we are speaking frankly, I'll tell you something else. She would cause trouble if she could. Don't ask me how I know—I just do. Call it intuition if you like—a feeling in my bones.'

He nodded. Heavens, she thought, in mild surprise, he's actually agreeing with me!

'Yes, I think you're right. I wish now that we had not gone—but these things happen,' and he shrugged. 'Your presence here would have been talked about even more if we had not. Pearl saw you in the car, that was the unfortunate thing, and the speculation would have been rife. So I did what I thought best. I regret if it causes you distress to have to pretend to be engaged to me—but it is only for a short while——'

'And then the engagement will be broken off,' she murmured. 'After we find the treasure.'

'Yes,' he nodded. 'Your ordeal will last only for a few weeks, and only when they—or others, come visiting.'

'Then I'm sure I can cope,' she answered. 'That's what's really worrying you, isn't it? That I'll let you down? Then I can assure you, you needn't. I've agreed to stay—and we won't go into that now —and I'll do my part. But it's no use me pretending it'll be simple. I've met people like Jeanne before in my job and I've learned that they are best avoided. I just thought it only fair to tell you so that I won't have to cope with her alone. Is she in love with you?' She could have bitten her tongue off at the question, because it was the last thing she intended to ask, but it came out almost of its own volition. And Bryce's face changed—fractionally— but it was enough.

'In love? I doubt if she knows what love is. She collects men like a Red Indian collects scalps. That is the sum of it. I represent a challenge to her, that is all. Someone who is immune. She does not like that.'

'I see,' said Kim softly. 'I see now what you meant about getting her off your back. The picture is very clear.' She smiled at him. 'So you're using me to do it, are you?'

'I told you that I regret——'

'Oh, come off it,' she cut in bluntly. 'You said yourself we don't need to pretend with one another, so don't try it now. You haven't got where you are by being soft with people——' she could see his face darkening, but she didn't intend to back down now. 'And I'm quite sure you don't give a damn about me—you've made *that* very clear—so don't keep saying how much you regret everything that's happened. Because I don't believe you do——' and then she stopped, breathless, because he looked as if he could strike her. Instinctively she moved back slightly, aware suddenly that she had gone too far, and he caught hold of both her arms and pulled her towards him.

'I would be silent if I were you,' he grated, his voice deep, almost husky. 'You have said enough!'

'You're hurting me,' she breathed.

'Not as much as I would like! That is the second time you have insulted me. I do not forget that.'

His eyes bored into hers, and she stood very still, because to struggle would be to enrage him still further.

'Then what are you going to do about it?' she asked, and tilted her chin with sudden defiance. 'Hit me or something? You could you know. You're big enough and strong enough—only it would give your friends even more to talk about if I appeared at the party with a black eye——'

'I do not strike women,' he said, quite softly, but with more emphasis than if he had shouted. 'But I have never in my life met one who could make me so angry as you——'

'Then we're equal. Because *I've* never met a *man* who could get me so mad——'

'No? Perhaps they keep away from you—with a temper like yours, I should not be surprised——'

'How dare you!' She wrenched herself free from his grasp. 'How dare you speak to me like that! *You*—who are using *me* as a shield to protect you against another woman—you're not a man at all!'

She had gone too far. But she knew it was too late as his arms tightened round her, two steel bands of incredible power, and his mouth came down on hers on an earth-shattering kiss that seemed to go on for ever until finally he released her. 'Now,' he said, 'say that I am not a man if you dare!' His eyes were dark, gleaming with temper.

Kim swung her arm up and hit him across his face as hard as she could.

'And that,' he said softly as he touched his cheek, 'is the third insult!' And he turned and went out of the room.

There was no Ann to wake her the following morning. Kim lay for a while wondering why the house was so silent. No sound, no movement—nothing. She looked at her watch, and it was nearly eight-thirty. Puzzled, she got out of bed and went to wash and dress. She put her swimsuit on underneath trousers and sweater and went quietly downstairs. Only a clock ticked somewhere in the distance and the little black cat ran up and rubbed itself, purring, against her legs. Kim picked it up. 'Hello,' she whispered. 'Where is everyone?' She had slept badly, and would have given anything not to be going diving that morning, especially not with the dark and angry Bryce. It was open war now; the smouldering tension had exploded into brief violence the previous night and she felt faintly sick at the memory of their scene in the library. If only ... But it had happened, and there was nothing she could do about it. And then she saw him, coming towards her across the sunlit hall from the direction of the kitchen, and her heart skipped a beat. She waited, holding the cat as if it might help her —keep her safe.

He wore a dark sweater and trousers and was unshaven. He looked tough, powerful—and even, to her sleep-starved eyes, faintly sinister. She trembled momentarily at the thought that she had dared to hit him, and then braced herself inwardly for what was to come.

'Gordon has driven Ann and Matthew to the station,' he said. 'I am preparing breakfast in the kitchen. He will soon be back.' His voice was cool, no trace of anger—or anything else there. He turned away and walked back from where he had come and Kim, having no choice, followed him. She sat down at the large pinewood table and put the cat down.

'Coffee?' Bryce asked without turning from the large gleaming cooker.

'Please. Nothing to eat—not if we're diving——' she faltered.

'Yes, we are diving. Gordon will eat when he returns. We will do so later.'

He handed her a heavy beaker full of coffee and pushed a sugar bowl towards her, then sat down with a beaker himself. 'And now we are alone we will talk.'

'Yes?' she said faintly. She swallowed some coffee.

'Yes.' Eyes cool under those thick level brows, face hard, jaw shadowed. She would not let him intimidate her. She lifted her chin slightly.

'About what?'

'About our work—this hunt. Personal dislikes will not enter into it. I trust I am making myself clear?'

'Oh, perfectly,' she answered. 'I feel just the same. Is that all you wanted to tell me?' She looked up and met his own cool glance with one of her own. Just for an instant—a mere flicker of time— something showed in his face. Then it was gone.

'For the moment—yes,' he answered. 'But no doubt there will be more to talk about before we go visiting again.'

'To Pearl's, you mean? You needn't worry, no one will guess——' she paused, and he finished the sentence for her:

'—that we are anything but lovers? I wonder. Do you think you can act the part?'

'I managed it yesterday, didn't I? They might not be my kind of people, but they don't frighten me. And as I'm here to stay I might as well make the best of it. I don't back out of *my* part of a bargain, I assure you.' She sipped her coffee slowly. Let him make what he wanted of that! If only he wasn't so disconcertingly male—so overwhelmingly strong-looking. Kim had met many different types in her journalistic work, but nothing had prepared her for a man like this, one who seemed to move through life with an easy careless grace—and yet who got precisely what he wanted, all the time. And that being so, she wondered briefly if his comment about a party had been accidental after all. She didn't imagine he was the kind to make a *faux pas*. Could it have been deliberately timed? But if so—why? There was absolutely no reason that Kim could think of—not one at all. She would not risk another argument by asking him. She needed time to recover from the previous night's first.

'Have Ann and Matthew gone on holiday?' she asked. That was safe ground, a perfectly normal question.

'For three days, to their married daughter's in Vienna. That is how they prefer their time off, every fortnight. I thought it would be necessary to have temporary staff while they are away, but I find that I can manage quite well alone. And especially so is it preferable at the moment, with the search going on. I trust Ann and Matthew implicitly, but I might have trouble with, say, a woman from the village. So——' he shrugged carelessly, 'we must look after ourselves, prepare our own food—Ann has left a lot of stuff in the freezer which only needs heating.' He smiled slightly. 'She fears we might starve.'

'Can you cook?' Kim said, wondering why she should want to know.

He seemed surprised at the question, then answered: 'Yes. I enjoy it. Do you?'

'I'm not very good, I'm afraid. But if you want me to do any, I suppose I could.'

He gave her a faint smile. 'I would not ask my—guests—to work.' The hesitation was very slight, but there all the same. Kim took a deep breath. There must be no more arguments at all. Because she always came off second best, and more than that, at this moment the atmosphere, while not exactly amicable, was at least not as tense and hostile as was usual when they were alone together. For some strange reason she wanted to keep it so.

'Then I can at least keep my room tidy,' she said, and tried a smile on him.

'That would be fine. Thank you,' and he gave her a nod of the head that was like a small formal bow. Heavens! she thought. In a minute I can see we'll be hugging one another! And, most oddly, a little shiver ran down her spine. She stood up, the coffee finished, because she didn't want to stay there with him any longer, and the cat sprang on to the table. Kim picked it up.

'What do you call it?' she asked, because she couldn't just walk out either.

'Kóshka,' and he grinned suddenly.

'That's the Russian word for cat, isn't it?'

One eyebrow lifted fractionally, faintly surprised. 'So, you know some words, yes?'

'A few, that's all.' And she didn't intend to tell him where she had learnt them. Some memories were painful. So before he could ask, she said quickly: 'But the dogs—I would worry——'

'It was the dogs who found him!' came the surpring answer, and at Kim's widened eyes, he actually smiled. Sometimes, she thought, he's almost *human*. 'They often bring back dead rats and mice on their nightly patrols of the grounds. We are used to that—but one morning it was a different offering. I was woken about six in the morning by their barking, and so I went down, thinking they had disturbed an intruder. Instead, just outside the back door I found this half frozen bundle of black fur, being licked by Valery, while Boris barked his head off. Yes, you are surprised. So too was I, I can assure you. They are hunters, and could easily have killed him—but they didn't. Kóshka was a mere kitten, more dead than alive, and I never knew where they had found him, but I brought him in, gave him warm milk, wrapped him in a pillowcase and left him in a box in the kitchen. And now here he lives. See. I will put him out now, it is time he should go, and you will see what happens.' He took the cat, who resisted momentarily, from Kim's arms, and went to the door and opened it. Kim, consumed by curiosity, followed him. He whistled, the two dogs bounded up, and he put Kóshka down. It was so funny that she had to repress laughter at what happened next. The two giant fierce-looking alsatians dived upon the small creature with tails wagging and evident signs of great pleasure. Kóshka stalked between them with dignity, apparently oblivious of the adoration, heading for a stone outbuilding some distance from the house and obviously not going to let anything stop him.

Bryce closed the door. 'The dogs sleep there,' he explained. 'Kóshka is going to see if there are any mice for him. So you see——' he paused, 'your worry is unfounded.'

'You like animals, don't you?' she asked.

He shrugged. 'They are useful,' he answered.

That was not what she had meant. 'But you brought in the cat—a stray——'

'Would you have turned it away, a living creature?'

'No, of course not. But——' and then she stopped, unable to go on, because they were on perilous ground again. How could she say: 'But you are hard?'

He was too shrewd—and quick—for her. Sometimes, she thought, he can read my mind. 'But I am not like you? No, that is clear, I am not. But I am not cruel to helpless creatures either. Or did you think I would be?'

Kim shook her head. What was the use? Every single thing either of them said to each other was sufficient to start the tension building up. She could feel it now in the room. 'I think I'd better go and get changed,' she said.

'Yes, I think you had better. Before you say something unfortunate, as seems to be the way of it when you and I are together.' So he knew it as well as her!

'That's right,' she answered as calmly as she could. 'I won't be long.' And she went out of the kitchen, but before she did go, she added: 'Thank you for the coffee, it was excellent.' Then she smiled as she left.

Everything was so different when they were by the lakeside at last. This was it—the beginning of the actual search that might or might not lead to a fortune. No one could tell. There was always an element of luck in any venture, even when careful preparations had been made, when nothing was left to chance. And, too, there was danger. They all knew it, and there were certain rules to be obeyed to minimise risk. Kim had every intention of obeying Bryce implicitly in the water, for he was clearly an expert from the way he had spoken, from the precise plans he and Gordon had drawn up.

The boat was an excellent craft, with powerful engines. Everything was aboard, and Gordon had an air of almost boyish excitement about him as they set out from the shore and the motor throbbed into powerful life.

'This is just the job!' he shouted, steering the boat with skill, eyes alight with an enthusiasm she knew of old. There had been a subtle change in him ever since her arrival, Kim realised that without Bryce telling her. And even if we accomplish nothing else, she thought, my trip will have been worth it for that fact alone. It was as if he had found a purpose in life again.

Their first day's search was to be on the far side of the Schwartzee. She could almost see the area in her mind after careful study of the map. She sat and looked around her at the costly equipment. Underwater camera—lights—air tanks—baskets on lines ready for when—if—they found what they sought. Bryce had missed nothing. She looked up at him, standing big, dark, and powerful beside Gordon at the wheel, laughing at something his friend had said. A knife glinted at his waist, a compass was strapped to the wrist of his wet suit, and she thought suddenly, almost with surprise, I'm going to enjoy this. Absurd really, because she disliked him intensely, but she sensed that underwater all enmities would vanish in their different world.

Then, interrupting her thoughts, he turned and called to her: 'We are nearly there. Stand up and we will attach our air cylinders.' Kim scrambled to her feet. The boat puttered into silence and rocked gently, and she stood there as he helped her adjust the heavy tank to her back. His touch was quite impersonal, deft and skilful.

And then they were ready, and standing at the side, and a tingle of anticipation filled her. 'I will go first,' Bryce told her. 'You follow me.' He gave Gordon a salute which was returned, with the words:

'Good luck to you both. I'll be waiting.' Bryce launched himself backwards in the water and Kim counted to ten, slowly, then with a brave thumbs-up sign to the waiting Gordon, she followed Bryce. This was it. The start of the search.

CHAPTER SIX

No sound, the whole world shades of blue, every movement graceful and unhurried, breathing easily and gently, Kim kept near to the dark shape in front of her as he melted through their new element, deeper and deeper, powerful, kicking outwards with flippered feet, a human fish that looked back to see if she was following, then went on with strong and graceful movements.

And then they reached the lake bed, which was littered with boulders, dark frightening shapes looming suddenly up in front of them. They were closer now, as if by instinct, and Kim saw Bryce turn and give a signal. They had worked out a system of signs. Simple underwater language where no speech was possible, and this was asking her if everything was all right. She returned in the affirmative. Air bubbles rose to the surface with every breath they exhaled—then Kim thought she saw something in that dark blue gloom, and she pointed, touching his arm as she did so. She saw his nod, and then he was off towards it and she followed, a small thrill of excitement coursing through her veins at the thought that perhaps this was it—how strange if they should succeed on their first attempt. How marvellous...

It was a rock, as big as their boat, not a plane, but a gigantic boulder that was wedged as deep and firmly as if it had been there since the beginning of time, and perhaps it had. Fishes swung away in alarm at their approach, slender black darts of speed, elusive, silent.

Then they were going on again, and Kim played follow-my-leader with the big dark Russian who was her partner underwater—and a different man from the one she knew in their other world. For he had kissed her.

Strange that she should think of that incident now, when she had managed to put it out of her mind altogether. Warm memory flooded her as she followed him, and he paused and waited, as if something had communicated itself to him, and Kim nearly collided with him. What was it? He couldn't have guessed, could he? But he was taking the knife from his belt, and she saw the long trailing underwater plant that could have trapped them if they had gone on. Graceful, deadly, powerful strands of weed that could wind themselves round an unwary limb and tighten so that you were helpless...

It was done, he put the knife away securely in its sheath and they skimmed on through the alien world they now inhabited, and Kim was free to wonder at that memory of his kiss. Why now? Why not before, when it had happened? Because she had put it so firmly out of her mind that it had been almost forgotten. Almost ... She had been kissed by other men, and some kisses she had enjoyed, and some she hadn't. And there had been one man who had been special. She had met him in West Germany two years ago—and he had taught her a few words, a few phrases in Russian, a big dark Hungarian who travelled Europe taking photographs to sell to the newspapers and magazines of the world. The only thing he had forgotten to tell Kim was that he was married, and when she found out she had said goodbye, heart bruised but not broken. And now she was immune, especially to big dark men—and more especially to this one—because they were all out of the same mould, and not to be trusted. She was glad that she had hit him. He had deserved it, and would not try again. But if he did ... Kim drew her breath sharply, forgetting where she was, and went momentarily dizzy —a foolish thing to do underwater, where breathing had to be regular and as controlled as other movements. A cramping pain touched her leg, and she braced the muscles instinctively, then writhed her body round and rubbed the rubber-clad limb.

Bryce was beside her, touching her, signalling— what is it? She pointed and flexed her leg, telling him as best she could what was wrong. But she must pretend it was all right, because he had his doubts about her, and she could sense impending anger if she was to hold him back in his quest. She gave him the 'all's well' signal, and he nodded. Then they were off again, searching, swimming, looking all the time, never still, never pausing, for there was a lot of water to cover, and a certain area to be done every day. And it would be done, of that fact Kim was quite determined.

There was no counting time in their world, no way of judging the seconds or minutes, which was why they both wore waterproof watches on their wrists. She saw him point to his, and frowned, puzzled, peered with difficulty at her own, and realized. Nearly two hours had gone—it had seemed like minutes. He pointed upwards and began the slow ascent that would return them to Gordon. And it had to be slow—there was danger in rising too fast. She let him set the pace, because in this she trusted him absolutely, and he knew precisely what he was doing.

The final stage; the wait below the surface, where light danced downwards in shimmering shafts, and then it was over. Their first expedition. Gordon laughed, and waved, and Kim waved in return, taking off her face mask and breathing in the clear cold air in a sudden surge of joy. The cramp struck again as she swam towards the boat, following Bryce who scrambled up the ladder and leaned down to help her.

She sat down on the deck, wanting to rub her leg, not daring to do so, and Gordon handed her a beaker of coffee and crouched down. 'What's wrong, lassie?' he asked softly.

Bryce was busying himself with their equipment. She pulled a face. 'A touch of cramp,' she whispered. 'Don't say anything, will you?'

'Och, it'll pass. You're new to it just now. It'll pass. I'll find you a couple of salt tablets—they'll do the trick.'

The coffee was hot and strong, and just what she needed, and she nodded gratefully, not minding anything. She had proved she could do it, that was all that mattered. She had proved that she was as good as him in the water, as fast and as capable. And she had seen something he hadn't. Even if it had only turned out to be a giant rock it had showed that she was alert to anything—to any signs of what they were seeking. It was enough. Kim was satisfied. She looked up when Bryce came over and was almost tempted to smile at him.

'So—you had cramp?' he said, and frowned slightly.

'Only a little. It's gone now,' she lied.

He didn't believe her, she could tell that. He crouched down, large and intimidating in his wet suit. 'Do you often get it?' he asked her, and she shook her head. She could see Gordon coming back with the two salt tablets and signalled with her eyes to tell him not to. Bryce looked round, then back at Kim. His lips widened in a brief, cynical grin.

'So—it is gone now?'

'*Yes!*' she said very clearly.

'Good.' He straightened up. Gordon handed him a mug of coffee and winked at Kim, all innocence. Kim stood up, and Bryce watched her, quite deliberately and coolly. Damn you! she thought. He could spoil anything, just by an inflection in his voice. Oh, how I hate you! she added to herself.

'No luck?' Gordon enquired.

'No.' Bryce shook his head. 'But it went well. I think, if it is agreeable to you, Kim, that we will combine breakfast and lunch as soon as we return home, and then return here at about two, while the light is still good.'

'That suits me.' She looked at him with a coolness to match his own. 'It's your party.' Gordon was lifting off the air cylinder, putting it down. He would check them afterwards, as he would all their equipment, for nothing must be left to chance.

'Aye well,' he said. 'Let's be getting back to the house.' And he went back to the wheel, leaving Kim and Bryce together.

'My party?' Bryce said in his deep voice. 'Is that an English expression?'

'Yes.' She turned away and gripped the rails as the motor began to throb.

'And what does it mean?'

She looked sharply at him. 'I would have thought you'd know. It means you're in charge.'

'Oh, I see.' He nodded slowly. 'I must remember that.'

'Yes, do.' She turned away again.

'Tell me,' he said, 'where did you learn your Russian?'

Her leg still ached with the aftertaste of the cramp, and she was trying to flex the muscles without him noticing, and his question was so unexpected that she caught her breath.

'A friend taught me,' she said briefly—dismissively.

'A Russian?'

She looked at him again. 'No.'

Bryce smiled, very slowly. 'So—I think you prefer me not to ask?'

'So—you are right,' she answered, mimicking his use of that first word. She saw the muscle tighten in his cheek, the hardness in his face. In a minute, she thought, he's going to tell me I've insulted him again—but I don't care!

'Forgive my rudeness,' he said softly. 'I did not think the question would distress you.'

'It doesn't.' She lifted her chin. 'It doesn't distress me one bit. I just prefer not to tell you, that's all. *If* you don't mind.' But she wished he would go away. She gripped the rail so tightly that her knuckles were white. The boat cut through the smooth sunlit water as it went back towards the shore, and Bryce looked down, then at her face, and without another word, turned and padded away barefoot towards Gordon. Kim let out her pent-up breath in a deep sigh. She was surprised to find that she was trembling.

The afternoon was a repeat of the morning. Kim took two salt tablets before going down, and kept free of cramp. They swam in the planned area for two hours, and then returned to the house. There were now two crosses on the map of the lake, a map which had been divided into nearly forty squares.

The phone was ringing as they went into the house, and Bryce went in his study to answer it, a room Kim had not seen, but was to do so within minutes, for even as she went up the stairs to change, he called her:

'Kim? It is for you—your grandmother. You may speak in my study—it will be quite private.'

'Oh. Thank you.' He opened the door for her, indicated the telephone, and then went out, closing the door again firmly. She seated herself at the huge desk and picked up the receiver.

Her grandmother's voice came across the miles as clearly as though she were in the next room. 'Well, you're a fine one! I've been waiting for a letter full of news from you—and who, pray tell me, was that gorgeous-sounding man who answered the phone?'

Kim began to laugh. 'One thing at a time, love! First, I've only been here a couple of days, and I intended writing tonight, cross my heart, only I can't tell you what we're doing because it's secret. How are you, anyway? You sound full of beans.'

'Hmm, I'm not so bad, dear. I've just had a card from Jack, which is why I've rung really—and to tell you off, of course.'

'I consider myself duly told off. What does Jack say?'

A moment's pause, a fumbling, then: ' "Tell my sister to pack her bags and come out and join me here. She'll get the best story ever—more in a letter——" That's all for you, but I thought I'd let you know. So you can't tell me *what* you're doing, but you can tell me *who* that was.'

Kim swallowed. What if he was listening? 'He's —er—our host. Gordon's and mine, I mean. We're all working together on something.'

'Yes, but *who* is he? He's not Austrian, is he?'

'No, he's a Russian. It's a lovely house, Gran, you'd love it. Enormous gardens, and two big alsatians——'

'Tch, never mind that! What's he like? Old, young, fat, thin?'

'About thirty-four, I imagine. He's known Gordon for *years,* and he's—well——' how did you describe a man like Bryce? 'Tall and dark—look, your phone bill will be *huge.* I'll write and tell you everything, I promise.'

There was a disbelieving snort that carried quite clearly over the ether. 'Hmm, well, never mind that. I'm more concerned with your welfare than my phone. Are you well? And happy?'

'Absolutely. Everything's splendid. Shall I give Gordon your love?'

'Do, dear. Tell him to write as well, when he's got a moment. All right, I'd better go anyway, I've got three friends coming round for bridge this evening. You know how it is. Bye-bye, Kim.'

'Bye-bye, love. Thanks for calling.'

She looked round the room as she put the telephone down. A man's room, plainly and simply furnished, yet with an elegance that spoke of money. Two comfortable leather armchairs in front of the fireplace. No fire was lit but the room was warm with the radiators that lined the walls, and the thick dark green curtains at the window ready to shut out the worst weather. Besides the desk, and wooden chair, there were several cupboards, a few pictures on the dark oak walls, and a framed photograph on the mantelpiece. Her survey of the room had taken Kim only seconds, but as her eyes reached the photograph, she stopped, and walked to it. Because there was something about it...

It was an old photograph, not large, but blown up from a very small snap, judging by the grainy quality to it. It was of a man, woman, and small child, all well wrapped up against a snowy background.

There was no one to tell her, but Kim knew that it was of Bryce and his parents. Knew it as surely as if it bore a label. She looked hard at it, taking in every detail with an intentness that surprised her. She couldn't take her eyes away. Whoever had taken the snap had captured a quality of despair in one instant of time, and had preserved it for ever. It shone out from the woman's eyes, that were as deep set as her son's. Bryce's eyes. Perhaps this was all he had to remind him of the past. Kim turned away, but she still saw the photograph in her mind's eye as she crossed to the door and opened it. She knew she would never forget it.

Gordon and Bryce were laughing in the kitchen when she went out to join them, and Gordon turned, face alight with fun. 'We're just choosing a menu for dinner,' he told her. 'Come and help us decide before you go and change. So far we've got roast chicken and all the trimmings or beef curry.'

'I don't mind,' she said, and shook her head. 'Who's doing the cooking?'

'I am. Why do you think we were laughing? Bryce doubts my ability.'

Kim smiled faintly. 'I'm sure you're very good. Anything will do me. I'm not very hungry as a matter of fact.' She looked at Gordon. 'Granny sends her love, and says you're to write when you can. I think I'll go and change, if you'll excuse me.' She didn't want to stay there any longer. She didn't know why.

'There'll be coffee when you get down,' Gordon's voice followed her. As she went upstairs, the telephone shrilled again. She listened for a moment, pausing on the landing, but Bryce didn't call her.

She towelled her hair vigorously dry, changed into black slacks and chunky yellow sweater and flat shoes, and went downstairs into the kitchen.

Bryce passed her a cup of coffee. 'Pearl has just phoned to ask us if we would like to go to a party at her house on Thursday,' he told her. 'If you do not wish to go——' he shrugged. Kim could see that Gordon was watching them. He must sense the atmosphere, she thought—but he says nothing. He's too wise. I wonder what goes on in his mind?

'Why not?' she answered lightly. 'As long as you'll both be there to rescue me if I need it.'

'I think Jeanne and Leo will be there too,' he added.

She looked up and met his hard gaze. 'They'd think it strange if we refused, wouldn't they? The only snag is, my hair looks a mess with all this diving—is there a hairdresser in the village?'

Bryce frowned. 'I do not know. Ann will return before then—she will know, but if not——' he paused.

'I can always do my own,' she answered.

'Your hair always looks super,' said Gordon.

'Why, thank you, kind sir,' Kim laughed. She didn't look at Bryce as she said it. 'The other snag is—I have brought a long dress, fortunately. It's just a plain white one, but I always pack it in case——' she frowned, 'but—well, it might not be good enough——' She hadn't realised there could be so many problems involved in deception.

'Go away and fetch it down,' suggested Gordon. 'Then we can see.'

'All right. But if you—we—are going to give this return party, I won't be able to wear it for that. I mean, *I* would, but as I'm your fiancée, it wouldn't be quite the thing, if you see what I mean.'

Bryce smiled very faintly. 'That is a problem we can take care of when the time comes.'

'I'll go and fetch the dress,' said Kim.

She had hung it in the wardrobe. It was of heavy courtelle, and packed like a dream, rolled up tightly in a corner of her suitcase, washable, with no need to iron, just the thing for a busy journalist —but perhaps not for a party where the women would all be dressed in *haute couture* originals, costing hundreds of pounds. Kim had no illusions about that. On a sudden impulse she slipped off her clothes and put the dress on. She had a nice warm tan from summer that was immediately accentuated by the white clinging material. It was a simply cut dress, very straight, with thin straps and low neck. She zipped it up at the back and went slowly downstairs, lifting the full skirt slightly, for it touched the floor when she had no shoes on.

She knew she looked good in it, because she *felt* good, and that was the most important thing, but she wasn't prepared for the reaction from the two men in the kitchen.

'My, my,' whispered Gordon, and gave a low whistle. 'Would you look at that now!'

Bryce looked at her, and for a moment she saw something strange in his eyes, quickly banished. Then he nodded. 'Yes, that is good. Have you any jewellery, Kim?'

It was her turn to smile. 'Just junk—you know, the chunky kind—but I wouldn't wear *that* here.'

'Will you wait a moment? There is something you could try. Excuse me.' There was silence when he had gone, then Gordon said, very softly: 'You look simply beautiful, Kim, there's no other way to describe it. Man, but you'll knock their eyes out in that.'

'In competition with Dior originals?' said Kim dryly.

'Yes, I know. But you've got something they none of them possess.'

Kim laughed. 'Go on! What's that? You'll be telling me next I should be a model!'

'Och, you can scoff. You've got a certain freshness no amount of money or make-up or Dior originals can compensate for. Why, Kim, you're beautiful!'

She kissed his cheek. 'And you make me believe you when you say it like that, but I don't kid myself. I'm not sophisticated like Jeanne, and never will be——'

'Och, who wants that anyway? I've met them all, and believe me, I know who I prefer.'

'And Bryce,' she said, very quietly, in case he was returning. 'What about him? Will I do justice to his image of a fiancée?' Her tone was dry.

'I saw his face when you walked in the room. Yes,' he answered.

'He hates me,' she whispered. 'We hate each other.'

Gordon looked at her. 'Aye? Is that a fact? I'd put it more mildly than that, child. I'd say you'd both got strong personalities that clashed, that's all. And you know something? You'll make a splendid——' and then he stopped abruptly because the door opened, and Bryce came in carrying a small box in rich rosewood, and put it carefully on the kitchen table.

'Let us see,' he said, 'if there is anything to suit you here,' and he opened it.

'My God!' said Gordon reverently. Kim just looked. It was like Aladdin's cave in miniature, a glittering assortment of brooches, necklaces, bracelets, and earrings lay inside the blue velvet-lined box, in complete disarray. Bryce put in his hand and scooped them out and laid them on the table.

'Now,' he said, and picked up a diamond collar that burst with rainbow brilliance in the overhead light. 'Try this on.'

It was heavy, five rows of tightly packed stones, and Kim took it from him with great care. 'It's not —it can't be——' she began.

'Real? Yes, it is. Let me fasten it for you, please.' His hands were cool on the back of her neck, cool and impersonal as he secured it. Kim put up her hand, as if to make sure that it was real. It fitted her slender neck perfectly.

'Earrings to match—and a bracelet. See.' He selected the matching items from the assortment on the table. Kim put the bracelet on her wrist where it sparkled fire in many colours, then clipped on the heavy earrings.

'May I go and look in my mirror?' she managed to say at last.

'Of course—but first, wait, please.' He was searching again. 'For the party, where you will be my fiancée, you had better wear a ring. There are three here, I think. One will surely fit.'

She knew immediately the one she wanted, and took it from his open palm. An antique gold ring with a superb diamond set in five claws, it slid on to her finger as if it had been made for her. She didn't even look at the other two.

'This one, please,' she said.

'You have good taste.' Bryce looked at Gordon. 'That is worth more than anything else.'

Kim felt a shiver run through her. 'But will it be safe?' she whispered at last. 'If I lost it——'

'Lose it? It fits, does it not? You will have it on only for the evening, and then I shall return it to the safe with the others.'

Kim held her left hand out, away from her, so that she could see the beautiful ring in perspective. She had never had any great longing to possess jewellery, but something, now, as she looked at her finger, stirred inside her. A heady sensation, new, and faintly disturbing.

'Then I will wear it,' she said simply. 'May I go and look now?'

'Yes.'

She pirouetted in front of her long wardrobe mirror, and the collar glittered and twinkled in the light, and the earrings swung gently with each movement and she thought: I'm getting vain, that's my trouble! Because she had never felt so absolutely *marvellous* in all her life. That being the case, she told herself sternly, it's time to take them off and change. Which she did, all except for the diamond collar, which Bryce had fastened on, and it defied all her attempts at undoing.

She went down to the kitchen again, carrying the bracelet, ring, and earrings, and said: 'Will you get the collar off for me, please? I don't know how it fastens.'

'Yes.' Gordon was busily chopping up onions by the cooker, face expressive with the effort not to shed tears. Bryce came behind her and he had to ease down the cowl neck of her collar. He was a mere few inches away, and she could feel his breath on her cheek as she turned slightly, suddenly breathless because her heart had started to pound, and she didn't know why, only that he was much too near . . . too near . . .

'C—can you manage?' she said, keeping her voice steady with an effort.

'It is difficult—I am sorry—with your jumper——' Then: 'No. Wait. Ah yes, I have it now.' His fingers, just for a brief moment, seemed to caress her neck. They were no longer cool, but warm—and almost gentle.

Kim felt the collar's weight disappear and moved jerkily away from him, and said quickly to Gordon: 'Let me help you.'

'Fine,' he said. 'The meat is already cooked. It's in the fridge. If you could get it out and cut it into small cubes, I'll prepare the stock.' Bryce went out with the box, and Gordon looked at Kim, grinning broadly. 'And the next question is—what's *he* doing with all that lot?'

'I wasn't going to—well, yes, all right. What is he doing with it?'

'Investments, my dear child. Better than all your money. And if he ever gets married, won't she be a lucky girl?'

Kim ignored that. 'They're certainly beautiful,' she said. 'Do you know, I felt marvellous with those diamonds on. And I don't really like jewellery. But just for a few minutes, I felt like a queen.'

'And you looked like a fairy princess,' he smiled. 'No, honestly,' earnestly, at her scornful expression. 'They'll not hold a candle to you, not one of them. I can't wait to see Jeanne's face——'

'Oh, Gordon, please don't say that! I hate deception, and this is what this will be, after all. It seems to have got out of hand somehow——' her voice trailed away, and she bit her underlip.

'Och, lassie, lassie! Not a bit of it! Where's the harm? Tell me that. We're not hurting anybody. Be practical for a moment. This hunt of ours is secret, and we wish it to remain so. Now, what do you think would happen if it was known that Bryce had a girl here, and no one knew anything about her? Jeanne would have been round like a shot, and maybe one or two others, and just imagine the speculations! We're nipping that in the bud right away by letting it be known that you're his fiancée, and there's an end of it. No one will search further than *that*. No one will dream why you're really here. D'ye not see?'

'I see—but——' she shrugged. 'Oh, I suppose you're right. You usually are. And I'm glad you're here, Gordon.'

'So am I, love, so am I.'

Kim looked at him with affection. He had a way, had Gordon, of smoothing things over, of making everything seem right, and natural. Almost everything—because she knew there was another reason for her uneasiness. It was so tenuous she could not even begin to put it into words. She certainly could not tell Gordon—because she didn't even understand it herself. But the image of Bryce swam into her mind at that moment. Bryce. Dark, puzzling Bryce. Why, she thought suddenly, should his nearness disturb me when I can't stand him?

CHAPTER SEVEN

THE pattern of their days was established now, and Kim knew that Bryce was well satisfied with her underwater help. She knew, because Gordon had told her. And after the Thursday morning dive, on their way back to the house, Bryce said: 'We will leave this afternoon clear for you to prepare for the party tonight.'

She looked at him, puzzled. 'What do you mean? I thought every afternoon——'

'But you wish to do your hair——' he shrugged, as if to imply that he didn't understand all the complications of party preparation.

'That won't take long,' she answered. 'The party doesn't start until nine-thirty. I can be ready in an hour—even less—even with my hair, and all the other things I need to do.'

He looked faintly surprised, and Gordon came to the rescue. 'What Kim means—I think—is that she's used to getting dolled up in no time at all. Right, Kim?'

She laughed. 'Something like that. Don't worry, Bryce, I won't let you down. I couldn't—not with all that jewellery on.'

'No. Nevertheless, we will leave it this afternoon. You have asked Ann about a hairdresser?'

'Yes. There isn't one. I'll wash my own hair. I've got shampoo and everything. It's naturally curly anyway, more's the pity.'

Gordon laughed. 'I thought that was considered an asset.'

She pulled a face. 'Well, yes. Usually, but you can't look very regal with a mop of curly hair, can you? I mean, all the others will have sleek hair swept back, all terribly gracious—see if they don't, and I'll be there looking like Shirley Temple!'

'Och, you exaggerate! You're fine, just fine as you are. Heavens, girl, they'd give their eye teeth to have hair like yours—I think you're just fishing for compliments.'

'I'm not,' she denied indignantly. 'You *men*!—you don't *understand*!' And she swept ahead of them, through the door and into the house, missing the look exchanged by the two of them.

There was a knock on her bedroom door as she was washing her hair in her own bathroom. 'Who is it?' called Kim, hair dripping.

'It's me, miss, Ann. I have a hair-dryer here if you want to borrow it.'

'Come in, Ann. I was just wishing I had one.'

Ann put it on the bed as Kim came out, turban-swathed, and smiled at the housekeeper. 'Sit down and I'll help you dry it if you like,' she offered. 'I've got curlers too, but I hesitated to offer those because your hair's naturally curly, isn't it?'

Kim grimaced. 'Yes. At this moment I wish it

wasn't.'

Ann laughed. 'You'd like it a bit straighter? No problem—I've got loads of grips and things. Do you want me to try something for you?'

'Would you? Have you got the time?'

'Mr Drovnik said I was to do anything you wanted. I'll go and get them. Won't be a minute.'

She was a very easy, pleasant person to get on with, Kim thought, as she waited for Ann to return. She plugged in the dryer and began to rub her hair at the same time. In two hours they would be leaving for the party at Pearl and Elmer's house. Kim was already suffering very mixed feelings about it. She sensed that in a way she would be the centre of attention, and for more than one reason. She was a new face—and she was, supposedly, the intended bride of a wealthy Russian. And she was an unknown, not of their social circle—and that third fact was, she knew, the most important. There was bound to be some resentment. Kim had met too many people on her travels to think otherwise. Her speculation was interrupted by Ann's return carrying a bag of grips. She was glad. It was no use brooding about it. It would not help.

The next hour was spent busily, and they both talked—and Kim, without appearing to do so, found out many things about Bryce that would help her build up a complete picture of the man. She had already made notes, and they were tucked safely away in her suitcase. There would be more now.

Ann did her best, seemingly enjoying her task, and when at last her hair was done, Kim looked in the mirror and smiled at the waiting housekeeper. 'I like it,' she said. 'Though how you managed to smooth some of those curls out I'll never know. Thank you, Ann.'

'It's a pleasure. I'll help you dress, then you won't disturb it, miss.'

Kim looked at the clock. 'Fine. I'll look my dress out. I've got some silver sandals too. While I'm getting them out, would you go and ask Mr Drovnik if I can have the necklace and other things? He's lending me some jewellery because the dress is very plain.'

'I'll go now, miss. He mentioned something about telling him when you were ready,' and she hurried out.

Kim laid the dress out on her bed, brought the sandals out from the bottom of the wardrobe, and threw the matching handbag on the bed. It was so small that it held only a handkerchief and lipstick, but at least it took scarcely any room in her suitcase. She sighed. If a message came to say that the party was cancelled, she thought, I wouldn't mind one little bit...

'Oh, miss, I hardly dared carry them. I was frightened of dropping them or something!' Ann's voice brought her back to earth, and the woman laid the fabulous assortment out on the dressing table and stood back to admire it.

'They are lovely, I know. Well, I'd better get dressed, then I can make up.' And Kim picked up her dress and handed it to Ann. 'Here goes,' she said.

She was ready. The last hair flicked into place and held with lacquer, her lipstick blotted, earrings firmly secured, everything perfect.

'Why, miss,' Ann breathed, 'you look absolutely fantastic!'

'Thank you,' Kim smiled. 'I don't feel *me*, somehow!'

Ann laughed. 'Never mind. You *are you*, whatever happens.' And that, thought Kim, was a profound remark, did Ann but know it. I am me, she repeated inwardly, and I may be practising a deception, but nothing can alter that fact—so why worry? In a few weeks I'll look back on this and find it an amusing episode. And it will all be over. Completely.

She smiled at the housekeeper. 'I'll remember that,' she said. 'And I'll let you know how the party goes, shall I?'

'Mmm, yes, do. Are we going down now? I think the gentlemen are waiting for you. They're having a drink in the lounge; they told me to tell you to join them if you will.'

'Thanks for everything Ann. Yes, off we go.'

She pushed open the lounge door and went in. Gordon stood by the drinks cabinet, Bryce was sitting by the fire stroking the cat. And as she walked in the room, he turned his head slightly, saw her, and stood up. She experienced an almost physical shock at the sight of him, and the picture he made was etched on her brain with an almost photographic clarity, with a sudden awareness that startled her. He wore an immaculate black evening suit, black bow tie in contrast to dazzling white shirt, and he was a tall, broad-shouldered, powerful figure of a man—and startlingly handsome. His raven hair gleamed dark and sleek in the overhead light, and his face had a bone structure that was almost classical. He bowed very slightly, almost with cynicism she thought, in her momentarily confused state, and said:

'You look perfect, Kim.'

'She looks stunning, you mean,' Gordon added, and said: 'Sherry—Martini—anything else?'

'Just a Martini, please,' she answered.

'Either Gordon or I will stay by your side all evening,' Bryce said. 'That is a promise.'

'If Karl is there, we'll need to,' said Gordon very dryly, and Bryce looked at him.

'Karl?' he frowned slightly. 'He does not bother me.'

'He'll bother Kim if he gets half a chance.'

Bryce laughed, but there was little humour in it. 'True,' he admitted slowly. 'But then he's not going to get the chance, is he?'

'Who is Karl?' asked Kim.

'A playboy—a womaniser—not someone you would wish to know.'

Kim widened her eyes. 'Mmm, he sounds interesting.' She took the drink from Gordon. 'Thank you.' Some imp prompted her to add: 'I gather you don't like him, Bryce?'

'No.' The answer was brief, dismissive. He looked at the heavy gold watch on his wrist. 'We will leave when you have drunk that. It will be after ten when we get there. I think we will leave at one. That is long enough to stay. You agree,

105

Gordon?'

'Och, you know me, I'm not a party man anyway. The sooner the better.'

Kim downed the Martini. 'Then I'm ready. Shall we go?'

Bryce lifted her coat from the chair and she turned her back as he eased it gently over her dress. 'Thanks,' she said, and smiled at him.

'The pleasure is mine,' he answered softly, and walked to the door to hold it open for her to go through. Kim lifted her head high. This was it!

I've been leading the wrong kind of life for years, she thought, as she sipped her champagne. This is where I really belong. Here, among the beautiful people, the golden ones, the jet-setters—and just for an evening, I am part of it all. There were probably fifty people at the party, and Kim, after her third glass of champagne, was decidedly light-headed. Bryce had not left her side for an instant, true to his word, and was the perfect partner, completely attentive, charming—a different man indeed from the one who had virtually blackmailed her into staying.

She turned to him. 'My glass is empty,' she said, and gave him a ravishing smile, because eyes were on them all the time. 'And I've decided that this is the life for me.'

'You have?' he cocked a cynical eyebrow. 'You must have drunk too much.'

'What do you mean? It's your world, isn't it? Don't *you* like it?'

He took another glass from a passing waiter and

handed it to Kim. 'It is not my world at all,' he answered calmly. 'Nor would I wish it to be. These people are not my friends. They are acquaintances, that is all.' The music was loud, and no one could overhear what they said, unless they were rude enough to hover over them, and both Kim and Bryce had pleasant 'I'm enjoying myself' expressions on their faces so that everyone assumed they wished to be alone, and left them—but watched. And I know why they're watching, thought Kim, for she had seen their reflections in a long wall mirror when they had come in, and her heart had contracted in sudden pain.

Because we look ideal together, she thought. We look—like lovers. A disturbing and distressing thought to have about a man she hated. And because he might read her mind, she said the first thing that came into her head: 'Where did you go this afternoon?'

He looked at her, eyes for a moment quite hard. 'Why do you ask?' he said.

'Because we're obviously not going to agree on your "friends",' she said the word with emphasis, 'so I thought I'd change the subject.' And she smiled brilliantly, tipsily, at him, and drank half her champagne in one beautiful swallow.

'I went out to see—some friends. Some real friends. That is all.' But her curiosity was aroused by his face, by the dark shuttering of his eyes, and she thought wildly: it's a woman—and was shot through with an intense wave of emotion which she had to hide, lest he knew.

'And you don't want to talk about it. I *see*,' she

said sweetly. 'Well, darling, hadn't we better circulate, before our smiles wear thin—or we have a fight, as is usual if we remain talking for any length of time.'

And then he began to laugh, a deep joyful sound that caused more than one head to turn. 'As you wish, my dearest. Come, let us—as you say—circulate. I think our hostess would like to talk. And Jeanne is looking our way.'

'Hmm, yes,' she murmured, as they made their way through the throng. 'Is that Karl she is talking to?' The tall blond man with wicked eyes had been regarding Kim with an expression that carried a very clear message. 'Because he fancies me.'

'Does he? How do you know?'

Kim gave him a very feminine look. 'Heavens, any woman knows when a man fancies her——' she hiccuped slightly. 'Oh, excuse me—darling. This champagne, you know!'

'It is better if you do not speak to him,' Bryce said, and took her arm.

'Is that an order?'

'If you like—yes!'

'The only orders you give me are underwater ones,' Kim told him sweetly, and then, because they were practically upon their hostess, 'Oh, Pearl, what a lovely party!'

'You're enjoying yourself, honey? So glad. Everyone was *dying* to meet you.' The American woman's teeth were nearly as dazzling as her jewellery, and she gushingly took hold of Kim's arm. 'Let me take you around and introduce you. Bryce——' this with an arch smile, 'you'll excuse us for a moment, dear, won't you?'

'Of course. Who could refuse you anything?' he replied, and smiled. But Kim knew he would be watching them like a hawk. Good, she thought, remembering Karl's vivid blue eyes, the way they had rested on her—not once, but several times. I'll teach *him* to give *me* orders!

The names didn't really register. The calculating looks did, as potently as the expensive scents that filled the room. Kim had on only lavender water, but she no longer cared. The champagne had gone to her head, and she smiled her prettiest and most confident smiles as she was introduced to these women and men who were not of her world —and never would be. And then she was talking to Karl—now deserted by Jeanne, who had seen Bryce alone and taken her chance to go over to him. Like a hawk descending on its prey, thought Kim.

She had had her hand kissed before, but never with such panache. 'Ah, that we should meet too late,' smiled Karl, with a wink intended for Pearl, an "I'm only joking of course" wink. 'My opinion of friend Drovnik's taste has soared since I saw you enter the room.' Then he noticed the ring that Kim wore—and she was aware of the slight change of expression. Very subtle, but it was there.

Pearl fluttered anxiously. 'Now, Karl,' she said, 'you're the biggest flirt out, you know that. Whatever will Kim think?'

Kim knew what she thought. Those vivid blue eyes, when seen near to, were a shade too close set, the glorious tan slightly artificial—in fact the man himself was not someone she would care to find herself alone with. Besides the charm, he oozed an overwhelming egotism. It showed in every move he made, every inflection of his voice, and she knew with a sense almost of shock that she liked him even less than her supposed fiancé. She looked round to see Jeanne on tiptoe whispering something to Bryce. And all of a sudden the party went sour on her. But there were another two hours to go before they could decently leave, so she smiled warmly at Pearl and Karl as he answered:

'I'm sure Kim is too happily engaged to take any notice of what I say. Hey, Kim?'

'That's true. Haven't you brought a girl-friend with you?' And she smiled.

'Alas, no one will have me!' he shrugged helplessly. And then another couple descended on them, determined to be introduced, and the subject was changed, and Kim was eventually able to make her escape with the excuse that she thought Bryce had signalled her. She left them talking and made her way through the noisy throng to join him. Gordon was there with Jeanne and Bryce, and he put his arm across Kim's shoulders and said quietly: 'Okay, love?'

'Yes, thanks, Gordon, I'm having a lovely time. Are you, darling?' This with emphasis and a warm smile at Jeanne. Heavens, she thought, I've never smiled so much in such a short time in my life.

'Lovely,' agreed Bryce. And Jeanne said:

'I've been hearing about your gorgeous ring, Kim. May I see it?'

'Of course.' Kim held her hand out.

'Ah, yes! Beautiful. You do not always wear it, though?' Jeanne's lovely eyes rested on Bryce, who answered:

'Not the other day. It was being made a shade smaller for Kim. She was nervous of losing it.'

How easily he lied! thought Kim. Without a thought. Her glass was empty. Gordon took it from her and handed her another.

'I don't think——' she began doubtfully, and Gordon said:

'Rubbish! Do you good.'

'But I've had enough,' she whispered. 'Really I have.' She must keep a clear head, she knew that. There must be no slip-ups, no words said that might arouse suspicion as to why she was really there, and then, as she saw Jeanne take another glass of champagne, Kim thought: Oh, what the heck! I'm not a child—and she lifted the glass to her lips with the knowledge that Bryce and Gordon were there to keep a very watchful eye on her, so everything would be all right. And there she made a big mistake.

She knew when she woke up that something terrible had happened, but the only trouble was—she couldn't remember what. Her head ached terribly, with a hammering insistence that refused to go away, and she couldn't think. Then she realised why she had woken. Someone was knocking at the door.

'Come in,' she managed to croak, and winced at the effort. It wasn't Ann who came in, but Gordon, carrying a cup and saucer.

'Oh! Gordon!' Kim sat up. 'I've just been try-ing to remember something, but I can't. My head is aching so much. But I've got an awful feeling of something *ghastly* happening——'

'Coffee, love—here, can you manage? That's it.' Gordon sat on the edge of the bed. Then he grin-ned at her. She knew that grin of old.

'Gordon? What is it?' she whispered, then took a swallow of the life-giving liquid.

'I don't know how much you can take in your delicate state,' he said, but his face belied his words.

'Gordon, for heaven's sake——' she began, and winced. 'Oh, my head!'

'Poor lamb. Hold on a moment, I'll away and fetch a couple of aspirins. Don't go away!' And he was gone.

It had something to do with Karl. That much she could remember, and a wave of dismay came over her as memories began to filter through. Karl —and Bryce—and her. It was like a mist beginning to clear and she frowned with the effort to recall— and then Gordon came in again and handed her a foil strip.

'No, wait, I'll do it. Your hands look none too steady to me.' He shook out the white pills into her hand. 'There you are.'

'I keep remembering little bits,' Kim said, 'but it's all a bit hazy. It involved Karl, didn't it?'

'It did. I'll tell you, and then it will all come back. Oh, boy, *what* a party that turned out to be!' He shook his head slowly.

'I'm warning you——' she began, and he held

up his hand.

'All right, love, I'll begin at the beginning. You began to feel slightly fragile—probably my fault for plying you with champagne—and whispered to me that you were going to find somewhere quiet to sit down for five minutes—and off you went.' He scratched his head thoughtfully. 'Mmm, and *then* —a short while after, Bryce, who had been well and truly cornered by Jeanne, managed to free himself and asked me where you were, so I told him. Only then *he* noticed that Karl had disappeared as well. "I'm going to find her," he said, and went out leaving me with Pearl and Elmer and some others. I had a feeling something was wrong, so I made some excuse, and left them all gossiping. That's one thing about these parties, there are too many people for anyone to be noticed —or missed. I went out, and then upstairs, and——' he stopped.

'Yes? Oh, *Gordon*—I'm beginning to remember! *Oh!*' Kim put her hand to her mouth.

'Yes? Well you tell me what happened before I got to the room, then I'll take it from there.'

'I went to the bathroom, and was intending to find a quiet room downstairs with a settee or something, just to put my feet up for five minutes. Anyway, I saw this *lovely* room upstairs, with a gorgeous bed covered in a huge furry rug type thing, and I thought—gosh, what wouldn't I give to sink down on *that* for five minutes. So I crept in, took off my shoes, and lay down.' Kim stopped and finished her coffee. 'Oh, Gordon, what happened next was *awful!*' She looked at him, dismayed and wide-eyed.

He said gently: 'I can imagine. Karl had found you, hadn't he?'

'Yes. I must have fallen asleep. And I dreamed this man was kissing me, and opened my eyes—and it was *him*. Karl! Then he started saying things like, he'd been waiting for me to go out, because he knew I felt the same way as him——' she stopped, horrified. 'Gordon, he thought I was mad about him!'

'He thinks every woman is, love, don't look so dismayed. Can you tell me what happened next, or do you prefer not to?'

'No, it's all clear now. I tried to push him away—and then I saw he'd closed the door and I was frightened, you can't imagine how frightened, honestly. He was terribly strong, and the more I struggled the worse he became—like an animal——' she shuddered helplessly.

Gordon patted her hand. 'All right, love. Stop now.'

Kim shook her head. 'It's all right. Because at that moment the door opened and Bryce came in.' She looked at Gordon. 'I've never seen anyone so angry. He just strode over—and sort of *lifted* Karl away, that's the only way I can describe it. He picked him up and flung him across the room.'

'And then I arrived at the door,' Gordon said, 'and saw what happened next. It would have been useless to try to stop him.'

'I thought he'd kill Karl,' she whispered. 'I was frightened.'

'So was I. I've never seen anything like it. But he

didn't, thank God. Karl is tough—very tough—but he didn't stand a chance.' He shook his head slowly. 'Och, I've seen some fights in my time, but that was a belter!'

'Gordon, how you can joke about it——' Kim's voice held a quiver.

'I'm not joking, love. Any man who does what he did deserves all he gets. What chance do you think you'd have had? Bryce taught him a lesson he needed.'

'But—the trouble it must have caused—fighting in another person's house—I mean, when Pearl and Elmer and all those others came up——' she lay back and closed her eyes.

'Och, it'll give them something to talk about for weeks. Do you not see? They may all be wealthy, but they live in a very small world. That's why they're always giving parties—it gives them something to *do*.'

'But they'll think that I——' she bit her lip.

'That you encouraged Karl? No. Because when you went out I had a word with Pearl, very quietly, told her you had a headache and had gone to be somewhere quiet for a wee while, and she was most concerned and wanted to go after you. But I didn't realise Karl must have overheard. Never you worry. She'll know the truth.'

'But Pearl is a bit of a gossip, Bryce said that——' she closed her eyes wearily. 'Oh, Gordon, I feel *awful*!'

'She knows what Karl is like, my child. Everyone does. He's had something coming to him for a long time. You honestly think anyone will consider you encouraged him? When they'd seen you and Bryce together? Forget it!'

He was comforting her, so why did his words make her so uneasy? That was something she couldn't, in her present state, fathom out. 'I'd better get up,' she said. 'We'll be diving soon. I must get ready.'

'Not this morning,' very gently. 'You're not fit— you know that.'

'But——' she looked at him, dismayed, 'I can't——'

'You can, and you will. Bryce sent me to tell you. The search is off for this morning. You stay in bed and get over your hangover.'

'I haven't got——' she began. 'Ouch! It's a *headache*, that's all.'

'Well, whatever it is, you cannot dive with it. I'll leave you now.' And he stood up and picked up the cup from her bedside table and moved away. A thought struck Kim.

'Gordon,' she said, 'was Karl badly—was he hurt?'

'I was hoping you'd not ask,' he grinned. 'Och, I'm only joking—he'll have a few bruises for a week or so, but the biggest dent is to his ego.'

'And Bryce?'

'Not a mark on him—well, maybe a wee bruise on his face, but that's all. Man, what a fighter! And I always thought he was non-violent.'

'Wait—don't go.' She had remembered something else that had been irritating her since the party—although she couldn't imagine *why*. 'Gordon, you know Bryce went out yesterday afternoon? Er—where did he go?'

'You're nosy—you know that?'

'Yes. Tell me, please, Gordon,' and she gave him a winsomely appealing look that had always had good results in the past. He moved slowly back to the bed, and grinned at her.

'You'll be surprised when I tell you—and I'll slaughter you if you breathe a word to a *soul*.'

'Cross my heart,' she promised. Her heart was beating faster. There was something in his voice, some quality she didn't understand.

He sat down again on the edge of the bed. 'He went to a children's home.'

'What?' She didn't understand. 'A children's home? I don't——'

'I said you'd be surprised. No one else knows either round here. It's his. I mean he finances it, keeps it going, and it must cost a packet too.'

She looked at him. 'For orphans?'

'There are some who stay there permanently, yes, and others from other countries—from refugee families. All sorts.'

'I can't believe it,' she shook her head, then wished she hadn't. 'And he doesn't tell anyone?'

'No.'

'Oh, Gordon,' she gave a huge sigh. 'I wonder why?' But she was seeing the photograph again in her mind's eye. That lost quality in their eyes—the helpless look—and she knew why, in part at least. She picked at the coverlet on her bed. 'I'm planning to write an article on Bryce.'

'*What!*' He stood up. 'My God, I wouldn't have told you if I'd known that!'

'Oh, it's all right—I won't put *that* in, although it would have helped fill the picture——'

'Listen, Kim, don't do it. He'll be furious if he finds out——'

'I intended showing it to him before I offered it to an editor, honestly.'

'I'd forget it if I were you. He'll say no. I know Bryce, believe me. When it comes to his private life, Howard Hughes is a positive extrovert in comparison——'

'But you don't *understand*. He'll make a fascinating story, don't you see?'

'I see your point of view as a journalist, yes. But I also see his. I'm sorry, love, but I know Bryce better than you, and my advice is—forget it. You'll spend hours writing this story, and he'll take one look at it and tear it up——'

They hadn't noticed the door, or heard the slight sound, until Bryce's voice came from the doorway: 'What is it that I will tear up, Gordon?' He stood there, formidable, larger than life, the big man who was host, fellow diver—and fighter. A dark bruise slashed his cheek, and he was unsmiling. 'Well?' he repeated. 'What is it? Can you not tell me?'

CHAPTER EIGHT

KIM took a deep breath. Gordon turned first to Bryce, then to her, but before he could speak, Kim did so.

'I was telling Gordon something that I planned

118

to do—and he was advising me against it, that's all.' She managed a careless shrug as if the matter was of no importance whatsoever.

'I see.' He looked at Gordon. 'There is a call for you from Vienna, on my study phone.'

'Thanks, Bryce.' Gordon half turned to go out, then stopped uneasily and looked at Kim. She pulled the covers up to her neck and smiled re-assuringly at him.

There was a moment's silence after he had gone, then she said: 'I'm sorry I caused you trouble last night.'

Bryce made a dismissive gesture with his hand. 'What is this I am going to tear up? A story—about me?' He must have heard more than they had real-ised. Kim bit her lip, feeling curiously defenceless sitting in bed.

'It was only an idea I had,' she said, with a touch of defiance. 'I thought your life story would make an interesting article, that's all.'

'Then you would be very well advised by what Gordon said—to forget it.' His eyes were dark and compelling. Not angry. Not yet.

'I was going to show it to you——'

'Were you?' He laughed. 'Do you expect me to believe that?'

'Yes.' She glared at him. 'I don't tell lies!'

'You are a journalist, are you not?' He made it sound almost obscene.

That stung Kim on the raw. 'I'd like to get dressed, *if* you don't mind,' she said angrily. 'I can't talk with you there. Would you mind leaving?'

'I shall stay here until I have your assurance that

you will forget your stupid idea,' he said calmly—maddeningly.

'Is that a threat?'

He shrugged. 'If you like—yes.'

'Why are you so frightened of me writing anything about you?' she demanded, feeling as if the ground was being swept from under her.

'Because my life is my own, and private. Not for you to discuss and write about. *That* is why, Miss Kim Dalby.'

I hate you, she thought suddenly. Oh, how I loathe you. And if you knew about the notes in my bag ... and she glanced across the room to where it lay on the dressing stool, as if he might guess. And he looked across at the same moment, and saw the handbag, large and somehow guilty-looking, and said softly: 'So? You have already begun, have you?' and strode over to it as if he had every intention of opening it.

'No!' she shouted. 'Don't you dare!' and dived out of bed, forgetting the cotton pyjamas she wore, oblivious of everything except the fact that he was not going to touch her property.

He picked it up and held it out of reach, tantalisingly. 'Give it to *me*!' she breathed, too furious to speak properly.

'Did you think I would open it? I was going to pass it to you for you to open and take out your notes——'

She tried to snatch the bag from him, but he was too tall. He moved it easily out of reach, and now his eyes glinted with something else. Amusement at her discomfiture? Furious, Kim grabbed his arm, trying to pull it down, and he held her with his other hand and said: 'Ah, ah, naughty! It is bad manners to snatch. Do you not know that?'

'You *beast*!' Incensed, she lashed out with her free arm and was jolted with the shock as it hit the solid muscle of his upraised arm. No one would be a match for him; he was built like a tank, she thought. 'Give me my bag at *once*!'

'When you stop behaving like a child, I will. Go and sit down. Get your dressing gown on,' and he picked it from the chair and flung it at her. Kim pulled on her warm blue nylon housecoat and felt immediately better. She rubbed her arm where it had struck his. It still tingled with the blow.

'Now, sit down.' She sat on the bed, and he handed the bag to her.

'That is better. Please pass me anything you have written about me.'

'And if I refuse?' She tilted her chin defiantly.

'I prefer you do not. I have no wish to use force, nor to search your handbag, because that is *your* private property'—the implication was obvious—'but if I have to do so, I will.'

She opened the bag. He meant exactly what he said. She handed him the notebook full of jotted sentences and odd words, and some in shorthand. 'That's all I've done,' she said.

He riffled through the pages, found the ones that were headed 'Bryce Drovnik', and tore them carefully out. Then he gave the book back to Kim. 'Thank you,' he said. 'And now, I suggest you forget your ideas and concentrate instead on why you are here. I assure you that is far more interesting than I am.'

'Maybe. But I can't write about that either, can I?' she said.

'When it is all over—yes, if you wish. And it will be your exclusive story.'

Kim brightened. But she wouldn't let *him* see. She gave a careless shrug. 'All right,' she said. 'May I get dressed now?'

'Of course. But we will not dive this morning.'

'Gordon told me so. But——'

'It is too late anyway. If you care to look at your watch you will see it is nearly eleven.' And with that he turned away from her and walked towards the door.

He was *impossible*. Aggressive, bossy—and now patronising. His words implied that she was letting them all down. She didn't know why or how, but that was the impression he managed to convey.

Stung to retort, she said quickly: 'If you hadn't made me drink all that silly champagne, I'd have been all right!' It was a childish thing to say—and she was to regret it immediately, for he paused by the door, gave her a hard level look, and said softly:

'You will be blaming me next for the fact that you flirted with Karl, yes? But you found out what happens when you play with fire——'

'Just a moment!' Her face was pink, she knew that. 'What on earth do you mean? Do you think that I——'

'Please do not bother with explanations now. I am not interested——'

'Then you damn well should be.' She stood up

122

and went across the room to where he waited. 'Just *what* are you implying? That I went off somewhere *with him*?' Her eyes sparkled angrily, her cheeks were on fire, and her carefully set hair was now a tumbled mass of curls after a night's sleep. She was not aware of her sudden beauty, nor would she have cared had she known, but the big man standing so accusingly before her saw, and his eyes darkened.

'Do you take me for a fool?' He spoke softly, but his voice was the more dangerous for that.

'You must be if you can say such outrageous things to me. How *dare* you!'

'You are a good actress. Very good.' And he smiled. 'But there will be no more parties while you are here.'

'That suits me fine.' She breathed hard, trying to regain a measure of calm. 'Although I can't see us getting invited to many if you go around fighting like some back-street brawler!'

'Back-street brawler? What is that?' He seemed almost amused—as if he knew.

'Oh, go to hell!' She turned away angrily, and he caught her arm.

'Never turn away when you speak to *me*.' It was there all right—hard arrogance. She stood still, knowing she could not fight him. 'I asked you what you meant.'

Kim looked up at him, seeing the contours of his face, the shadows, the deep-set eyes—and the bruise. And she smiled slightly.

'At least you didn't get off completely.'

'Nor did your—admirer.' The scorn he managed

to put into that last word was overwhelming.

'Then you must be well satisfied. Don't think I'm stupid enough to imagine you fought him only on my behalf,' she retorted. 'You loathe each other. I'll bet I was just an excuse. I hope you apologised to Pearl.'

'Of course. I try to behave myself as a guest.'

She began to laugh at that, and eased her arm free. 'Oh, that's funny! So it's normal to have fights at parties? I'm glad I'm not going to any more. You can sort out your own problems with Jeanne in future, when I'm not here—though you didn't seem to be trying all that hard to get rid of her, from what I saw!' And she gave a sharp nod, as if to say, get out of that! And the next moment something very surprising happened. Bryce put up his hand—and touched her cheek, quite gently.

'They burn like fire, my little wild one,' he said. 'Do they burn with temper—or jealousy?'

'What!' the touch of his hand disturbed her more than she cared to admit. 'Me, jealous? Don't make me laugh!'

He nodded sagely. 'Ah yes, then it must be temper. Forgive me.'

'Will you leave my room?' Kim had had enough, in more ways than one.

'Perhaps I had better.' He stood there, looking down at her. And she didn't understand the expression on his face. It was, if possible, slightly more disturbing than his touch had been. Then, without another word, he turned and walked out of the room.

Fully fit and determined to show Bryce that the morning's encounter had not upset her one little bit, Kim dived and swam her best that afternoon. They were in a deeper part, and he carried a powerful torch that lit the eerie underwater gloom as effectively as a car's headlamp would do. She tapped his arm and dived off at a tangent because she had glimpsed something, but it turned out to be the remains of a boat that had somehow become wedged in rocks. A piece of rotting wood floated lazily towards the surface and vanished from their sight. Tiny fish darted away in fright, and Kim gave a shrug. Bryce swam away, and she followed. It was a different world all right—and even more so at depth. Kim's ever-vivid imagination was at work. Any minute now the hulk of the plane could appear ... and she wondered, not for the first time, what Bryce intended to do with the treasure once he found it. Keep it? That had been her first thought, but his words in her bedroom that morning had caused her to think again. For he had said that she could write about their hunt—if she wished—afterwards. He surely would not have done so had he intended breaking the law. She looked at the dark powerful shape swimming strongly in front of her. Sure and capable in every move that he made, no wasted energy, as much at home in their new world as any fish as he was, she could not but admire his skill underwater. Gordon would surely know about the treasure. She would ask him some time...

He was slowing, treading water, waiting for her. Kim's heartbeats quickened. Had he seen something she had not? But he was pointing to his watch, and then upwards. The two hours had gone as swiftly as minutes. She nodded her acknowledgement and Bryce switched off the beam, and the darkness filled their world again. An eerie blue darkness. She knew quite suddenly that she would be frightened if she were alone.

A slow leisured rising, the more important because of the increased depth, and Kim followed Bryce, as she always did. His instinct was sure, his timing impeccable. Too fast an ascent and there was the danger of becoming ill with decompression sickness—the bends. Decompression chambers were kept on large boats from which deep sea diving took place, and in there stricken divers could decompress artificially. There was only slight danger at their depth, but caution cost nothing, save a little extra time in the ascent. The final pause below the clear surface of the lake, and then Bryce checked his watch and gave Kim the thumbs-up sign. How different he was now. How difficult to connect with the hard-eyed, disturbing bully of that morning—or the stormy fighter of the previous night's party. For Kim suddenly remembered, as if in a vivid picture, the grim determination on his face—the dark explosive temper that had swept him into swift retaliatory action. As she broke surface, she realised with surprise that it was the first time in her life that any man had fought over her. Underneath her mask she stifled a grin, thankful no one could see. In a week it might seem almost funny . . . But it didn't yet. It was still too near, too painful.

126

Bryce reached one strong arm over the side of the white boat. Kim grasped his hand and was pulled up on deck. She took off her mask.

'Thanks,' she said.

'No luck?' Gordon shouted.

'Nothing.' Bryce walked away from Kim and she unbuckled the weighted belt and kicked off her flippers. It was easier to sit down before you took the air tank off.

The two men were talking, and she watched them, perfectly content to just sit there, relaxing after the strenuous activity of the past two hours. She was as much caught up in it as they were, she knew that. And more especially since she knew she could write about it. Oh, for her camera! There was one on the boat, a heavy underwater contraption with which Bryce would photograph the wreck when—if—they found it. She wondered if he would let her have any prints if so. The better time to ask would be then—not now. The climate was not right for asking any favours from him; their brittle dislike coloured everything—and then she took a deep breath. Dislike one another they might, but one thing was certain; life had never been so *vital*, so worth living as it had been since she had come here. Even on her most interesting assignments, when she had been on the trail of some fascinating story, something had been missing. Yet here—since living at Bryce's house, Kim had found an element of conflict that had given life an added dimension, an added colour. That was the word—conflict. It came down again, she realized, to their basic clash of personalities. And she shivered slightly at the thought. Did it affect him too? She watched him waiting for Gordon as he poured coffee from the huge thermos jug, big, dominating the scene—as gentle as a panther waiting to pounce. And then she knew too something that she had denied ever since their first meeting. He was devastatingly attractive. No need to wonder why Jeanne couldn't keep away—nor the others at the party whose eyes had stayed on him when they need not have. Many women, Kim had seen them, wealthy, assured, polished—they were not immune to him. But I am, she thought. I can admit that he is attractive, that he has a certain magnetism, but thank goodness I can do so in an impersonal way. He doesn't affect *me* at all. And with that reassuring thought, she smiled a little secret smile to herself.

Gordon echoed it with his own as he came over. 'You look mighty pleased with yourself,' he said. 'What's the joke?'

'Nothing,' she assured him airily. 'Nothing at all. I'm just enjoying life, that's all.'

'Hmphm!' he nodded. 'I see.' And for a moment —just a fleeting moment—she wondered if perhaps he did.

On Saturday Gordon took Kim into the village to buy some flowers, and then up to the churchyard to see her father's grave. On the way there he said: 'Bryce had an invitation for us all to go to another party tonight, but he turned it down.'

She sat beside him clutching a bunch of roses, and turned her head to look at him, because there was hidden amusement in his voice.

'Where?'

'Och, some couple who were at Pearl's. You've caused quite a stir one way or another since you came, you know that?'

'It wasn't my fault about——' she began hastily.

'Och, I know fine it wasn't, but you've caught their imagination. Beautiful young English girl suddenly appears on the scene and whips one of Austria's most eligible bachelors from under their noses. Man, it's giving them something to talk about!'

Kim listened to his words in growing dismay. It had seemed such a foolish, trivial thing at first, that idea of Gordon's. Now it was snowballing out of all proportion. 'Oh, Gordon,' she said, 'what can we do?'

'Do?' he sounded puzzled. 'Why, nothing, lassie. It's only a seven days' wonder. There'll be some new gossip next week, I don't doubt.' He gave her a reassuring grin. 'Don't look so worried. I wouldn't have told you if I'd known. I thought you'd see the funny side——'

She nodded. 'I suppose you're right. But Bryce— I mean, when I've gone home again—won't he have an awkward time explaining——' she faltered.

'You're worried about him?' he laughed. 'Never worry about a man like Bryce. He doesn't give a damn for anyone's opinion.' No, she thought, I don't suppose he does. She shook her head faintly.

'You don't understand. It's not *that*. It's——' but she wasn't sure exactly what she did mean.

Only that she felt, for some obscure reason, very confused. 'Oh, I don't know, Gordon. It all seems so artificial somehow, us pretending to love one another, putting on an act. I didn't really enjoy that party, you know. And I'm glad we're not going to another one.'

'That's why he turned it down,' he said softly.

'You mean—he knew?' her heartbeat quickened.

'Aye. Och, don't get me wrong. You took the part superbly. It would have fooled me, had I not known the truth. But we were talking afterwards, and he said it wasn't fair to you——'

'But I thought you said he didn't care about anybody——'

'Ah yes, not *them*. Not at all. But you're different. You're here to help him in another way.' His words were having the oddest effect on Kim. She buried her face in the flowers and breathed in the sweet fragrance.

'So I won't be wearing the ring again,' she said at last, with an attempt at lightness. 'Pity, I quite liked it.'

He laughed. 'That's my girl!'

'Did he tell you what happened about that story I was writing?' she asked.

'The morning after the party, when he came into your room? No, I was meaning to ask you about that. I gather he doesn't like the idea.'

'You could put it that way,' she agreed dryly. 'He made me give him the notes. I thought he would have told you.'

'No, but I'm not surprised. I'm sorry, Kim.'

She shrugged. 'It doesn't matter. He told me I

can write about the treasure hunt—afterwards.'

Gordon gave a low whistle. 'Did he now? That's something.'

'Yes, I know. That's why, in a way, I don't mind about the other. This should be far more interesting.' She paused. They were nearly at the churchyard now; she could see the white church spire rising in the distance, coming nearer. There was just time. 'Gordon, if and when we find the plane and its contents—what are you going to do about the treasure? Keep it?' It was suddenly very important to find out. And he seemed to sense this, for he turned his head and gave her a slow smile.

'He is going to return it intact to the museum it came from. Did he not tell you?'

It wasn't the answer she had expected, but she didn't know why. 'I see.' She took a deep breath. 'He must have a special reason.'

'Maybe—but he's not told me. And I don't care. It's sufficient for me to be in on it. There will be a reward, of course, from the insurance if not from the museum—but that's not my main consideration, nor is it his. I would do anything for Bryce. He once saved my life.' Gordon shrugged. 'And I never forget a good turn—not one like that, anyway,' and he grinned boyishly.

'Oh, Gordon, I didn't know.' Things were getting more confused by the minute. Kim felt as if she had strayed into some Alice in Wonderland situation, where time, sound, and colour merged into a complex maze—with her in the centre of it.

Gordon stopped the Mercedes outside the gate, and they got out. Walking slowly up the path, he said: 'I've never told anyone before. It was—oh, ten or eleven years ago, when Bryce would be in his early twenties. We were on a dive, similar to this except it was in the sea off a Greek island. Quite simply, I went a little too deep—and you know what can happen sometimes—nitrogen narcosis.' Kim nodded, her face solemn. It was highly dangerous because the victim was not aware that there was anything wrong with him, and would begin to act almost as though drunk, owing to the increasing amounts of nitrogen being absorbed by the system under the intense pressure. Some divers had been known to rip off their masks, because in their fantasy world, caused by the nitrogen, they believed themselves to be able to breathe in water.

'I must have been in a bad way. There were four of us on the trip, looking for the wreckage of a Greek ship sunk thousands of years ago, reputedly full of fabulous treasure. We never found it, incidentally—but I read in a paper a couple of years back that an Italian team had—anyway, where was I? Oh yes, well, the others told me what happened afterwards. Apparently I had started acting strangely—I don't remember a thing, of course—and one of them saw me take my mask off and start thrashing around wildly as if I was fighting off a giant octopus or something—and Bryce was nearest to me and immediately swam to me and pushed his own air nozzle in my mouth—and then had to knock me out because I was fighting *him*. Anyway, to cut a long story short, he carried me to the surface—sharing his air, which must have been well nigh impossible—having to hold his breath and snatch air as quickly as he could, because of course I would just go on breathing normally, being unconscious.' He stopped, his eyes far away as he relived the past. 'And he had to keep stopping at each stage, to avoid the bends, *and* he had to keep my nostrils pinched——'

'I don't believe it——' breathed Kim, horrified. 'How on earth could he manage?'

'I don't know, lassie, but he did. And gave me artificial respiration when he'd dragged me ashore. Then he collapsed.' He shook his head in wonderment. 'I wish I'd seen it! The others tried to help, of course. But it was Bryce who did it, single-handed, and I'll never forget it as long as I live.'

'No, I can see that.' She wondered how much more there was to learn about that man Bryce. And then she saw the simple grey headstone—and he was forgotten.

'Oh, Gordon, someone must do a lot of work here. The whole place is beautiful,' she whispered. There were many graves, all neatly tended, with simple crosses or headstones and inscriptions, and all with flowers growing round, and carefully trimmed grass.

'Aye, it is. I'll away to the church and see can I find a vase or something for those roses.' He wanted to leave her alone for a few minutes. She watched him go. There was an atmosphere of great peace surrounding her. It was a cold day, a clear pale sky overhead, and a slight wind rustling the flowers, and distantly, birds singing in the trees. And Kim looked at the resting place of her father, and tears welled in her eyes.

She sat down on the grass and let the whole calm atmosphere of the place wash over her. Memories of childhood came flooding back unbidden, some happy, some sad. But her father was here, where he would have wished to be, in his beloved mountains. She looked at the roses, and touched a petal gently. Simple enough, yet they said a lot. And when Gordon returned, she was quite composed again.

They took the return journey slowly, neither of them talking much, both engrossed with their thoughts. As they neared Bryce's house, Kim touched his arm gently. 'Thanks for taking me,' she said.

'Och, that's all right. Any time you want to go, just say.'

'I will.' He drove the car round to the back, and stopped. Bryce was opening the back door, walking towards them. There was something about him ... Kim looked up sharply as he opened her passenger door. 'What is it?' she burst out, knowing something was afoot.

'You have a visitor,' he said.

'Me!' She slid out hastily. 'But who—I mean how——'

'Your grandmother,' he answered. 'She has come on a surprise visit,' and in a strange way, it seemed as if he were almost amused.

CHAPTER NINE

It was Gordon who took charge. 'Well, don't stand there gaping, lassie,' he said, shaking Kim's arm. 'Let's away in and say hello!'

'Yes, yes, of course.' She allowed him to lead her indoors, through the warm kitchen where Ann was preparing a meal, along and into the lounge. And Florence Dalby turned from the window where she had been standing and came forward to hug Kim, who was just beginning to get her breath back from the sheer astonishment at it all.

'Gran, how lovely to see you! But how——' she stood back to look at the tall elegant figure, immaculately coiffed, dressed in a rust-coloured tweed suit that would not have been out of place at a Dior fashion show, and shook her head slowly in amazement. 'How did you get here?'

'I flew, my dear, quite on impulse. Flew to Vienna, booked in at a hotel, and then took a train. Only your *dear* Mr Drovnik has insisted I stay here —isn't he *sweet*?' And Florence Dalby smiled a smile that Kim knew of old. She looked round anxiously at a sound, but it was only Gordon coming in to greet his friend. Kim stood back as they embraced, her still bemused mind working at speed. Granny was *here*. That was a fact. It was quite possible that it had been simply on impulse. She was like her grandson Jack in that respect. But, thought Kim, you and I will have a little talk later. Because I know you of old, and I saw your smile.

Her thoughts were interrupted by Gordon. 'Doesn't she look well, Kim?'

'Yes, as always.' Kim smiled warmly at her grandmother. It was good to see her, very good—and Bryce had asked her to stay. The Alice in Wonderland feeling returned more strongly. The next thing, she thought, is for Jack to walk in and say he was just passing, and he's found a plane in the lake, and the picture will be complete.

'What a beautiful house! I was saying to Mr Drovnik——'

'Bryce, Mrs Dalby. My name is Bryce. Please do me the honour of calling me that.' He had come in very quietly.

'I should be *delighted*!' She smiled at him, and Kim thought: she's quite taken with him. I bet she thinks he's lovely. 'I was just saying how much I like your house. Those pictures—ah!' She held up her hands.

'I am happy that you like them. There are more I can show you later when we have eaten. But first, I will go and collect your luggage from the hotel in Vienna,' and he smiled at her.

'But, my dear M—Bryce. I can't allow you, I'm sure I can manage—after all, it is just a *fleeting* visit——'

'I insist. The journey is no trouble at all by helicopter.'

'Helicopter? How fascinating! Do you know, that's the only thing I've never travelled in? How absolutely marvellous! May I have a little peep?'

'You may come with me if you wish, Mrs Dalby.' Her grandmother's face was eloquent. She positively glowed, thought Kim. I hope I'm half as active when I'm sixty-five...

'I can't believe it. Kim, this is too much! Oh yes, Bryce, I'd love that. Are we to go now?'

'If you are ready, yes.'

Mrs Dalby swept her copious handbag and gloves from the chair. 'Say no more. *Au revoir*, my darlings—or should I say, *auf wiedersehen*.' And with a warm tender smile at both Kim and Gordon, she sailed out of the room, followed by Bryce, who looked, for the first time, faintly bemused.

There was silence for a few moments, then both of them burst into helpless laughter. 'My God,' said Gordon, when he was at last able to speak, and wiping a tear from his eye, 'I do believe our Florence has made a hit with Bryce.'

'Did you see his face?' giggled Kim. 'It was worth it just for that. He looked as if he'd been hit on the head with a sandbag—kind of dazed.'

'Well, she can be a bit overwhelming,' agreed Gordon dryly. 'I mean, we've known her for years and are used to her, but he, so to speak, suddenly finds her standing on his doorstep, unannounced, right out of the blue——' he shook his head. 'Why, it could take him days to recover!'

'Mmm,' Kim thought about that. 'Just as long as she doesn't start on her pet theories while he's piloting the helicopter. He may just decide to tip her out over the Schwartzsee.'

'Och, she wouldn't——' then, faintly alarmed: '*Would* she?'

'You know her as well as I do, Gordon,' answered Kim. 'She just might.'

'We'll know when they return. You know, Kim, I've been involved in many a long discussion with your dear grandmother when she's been advancing some new aspect of one of her theories on life—be it politics, religion, philosophy, or whatever—and I've never yet come off best. But Bryce——' he shook his head. 'Bryce is a different kettle of fish. It will be like—like——' he stopped, clearly at a loss for the right words.

'Like the irresistible force meeting the immovable object?' suggested Kim dryly.

'Aye, just that. Precisely. Och, deary me, what will happen then?'

'We'll soon see, won't we?' she said.

And see they did, soon after dinner that night. It was, reflected Kim, like the continuation of a conversation in which she and Gordon had had no part, for when the two returned from Vienna they were animatedly talking, and had only stopped as dinner was served.

Kim looked at Gordon, and their eyes met across the comfortable lounge in which they were sitting, as Florence Dalby said to Bryce: 'To get back to your argument about unidentified flying objects——' she paused to put Kóshka on the carpet, and Kim scooped the cat up, glad of the opportunity to hide her face, lest it give her away. She was struggling not to laugh. 'I love cats, but I'm allergic to them,' she smiled apologetically at Kóshka, in case she had hurt his feelings. 'Now, you were saying before about my ideas on U.F.O.s— what exactly *was* it you were saying?'

'I'll take the cat out to the kitchen,' Kim muttered, and fled. She knew what would come next, and needed time to compose her face. Everyone loved Florence Dalby, for she radiated an irresistible charm, a charisma, but her words had given her away. She had said: '*your* argument,' to Bryce, which meant only one thing—she and he clearly didn't see eye to eye on the subject of flying saucers. Which meant that the rest of the evening would be anything but dull. Too many people underestimated Florence Dalby's intelligence because of her deceptively gentle appearance, and then found themselves wallowing helplessly in her sea of logic.

I wonder, thought Kim, as she returned to them after leaving Kóshka with Ann in the kitchen, if anyone can reduce Bryce Drovnik to a gibbering wreck? I wonder if he's ever come second best in anything before? She felt almost sorry for him.

It was better than any party, both she and Gordon agreed several hours and several drinks later when they were both left temporarily alone. Bryce and her grandmother were in the library searching for an old book on the subject of extra-terrestrial life. Gordon raised his glass. 'Here's to us,' he said, 'interested spectators in a marathon debate that could possibly go on for ever. Och, what wouldn't I give to have had a tape recorder going! Your grandmother would do well in the Oxford Debating Society. She's nearly convinced *me*—and I've never believed in the damned things before.'

'I gave in years ago,' Kim confessed. 'If she says there are little green men watching us, then there *are.*'

'And Bryce——' Gordon shook his head, bemused. 'Oh, my, I've never seen him enjoy himself so much.'

'Do you think so?' asked Kim anxiously. 'I mean, she is an uninvited guest—I'd hate to feel——'

'Och, not at all! He'd not have asked her to stay if he'd not taken to her straight away. He can sum people up in a flash, never you fear.'

'But she's *my* grandmother. Nothing to do with him at all. I can see they're getting on fine, but I feel guilty about her coming here——'

'Then don't! He's probably never met anyone like her before. It's doing him good. Don't worry, Kim. I'd be the first to agree with you—after all, I'm responsible for *you* being here as well—but he's found someone on his own intellectual level for the first time in years, can you not see? They're getting on like a house on fire. Leave them be and stop looking so concerned. Your grandmother can look after herself, and so can he—and may the best man win.' They raised their glasses in a silent, heartfelt toast. And the subjects of their discussion entered the room again.

Extra-terrestrial beings having apparently for the moment been abandoned, Florence Dalby was saying:

'My dear Bryce, I won't say a word. I think it's utterly fascinating. But you won't let me dive? Am I too old or something?' And Kim saw Bryce look at Gordon in silent appeal. He's told her, she thought in silent wonder. He's told her about the hunt, and she wants to join in. I *don't believe* it!

'You can't swim underwater, Gran,' she said. 'You must know that.'

'But I can swim, can't I? Surely there's not much else to it—except learning how to breathe properly, and I'd do that in no time.' And she gave Bryce a winning, winsome smile. Any minute now, he'll crack, Kim thought, and I'll be here to see it. It was quite a pleasant feeling.

'Mrs Dalby,' he said, 'I promise I will take you in the lake tomorrow if you wish—provided you can get into Kim's suit. But the diving is different. We work quickly, and quite far down sometimes. Kim is an expert, but I'm afraid I could not allow you—' he shrugged helplessly.

'It's quite all right, of course it is. And I accept your invitation, Bryce. Just to try it, that will be enough. I just thought—if I could have *helped* in any way——'

'You are very kind.' He looked as if he meant it—and faintly relieved too. She knows when to give in gracefully, does my grandma, thought Kim. It helps her win other—more important—battles.

'Tell me,' Florence Dalby began, seating herself comfortably on a settee and accepting a drink from Gordon, 'I'm sure you've plotted the lake very thoroughly, and are going over it systematically, but couldn't you hire one of those underwater detector things that they have on submarines? Asdic, I think it's called. I mean, wouldn't you think they'd make a miniature version for treasure-hunters such as yourself?'

They were off again. Kim looked at her watch as she stifled a yawn of pure tiredness, and discovered that it was past midnight. No wonder she was sleepy! The evening had passed swiftly. Her grandmother looked as fresh as ever, and so did Bryce, but she and Gordon were exhausted. And it was her grandmother, as if sensing this, who said:

'Gracious me! Am I keeping you all up?'

She was reassured by Bryce that indeed she was not. It gave Kim the opportunity to say goodnight —at which Florence Dalby herself rose and said: 'If you don't mind, Bryce, I really think I ought to retire now—but I'd just like to say that I can't remember when I've enjoyed an evening so much. Truly.'

Ann had prepared a room next to Kim's for her grandmother, and Kim followed her in, watching as her grandmother kicked off her shoes with a magnificent sigh of relief. 'Ah, that's better. Do you know, dear, I could have gone on talking all night with you all—isn't he absolutely adorable?'

Kim gave a wry smile. Adorable? Could anyone have ever used that word to describe Bryce Drovnik before?

'It must be a mutual admiration society,' she said. 'He seems to find you equally fascinating.'

'Mmm—well, yes, that's as maybe. But it's you I'm concerned about; do I detect a certain edge to the atmosphere whenever you speak to each other?'

'Is it so noticeable? We don't particularly like one another, that's all.'

'That's *all*! You must be blind, girl, if you can't see what an attractive creature he is! Heavens above, he sounded like the answer to a maiden's prayer on the phone—I imagined he'd be an awful let-down when I arrived, and instead what do I see? Why, a huge chunk of glorious manhood positively oozing sex appeal! Can this be my own granddaughter talking?' She sat on the bed and unbuttoned her jacket.

'You'd get on well with Jeanne,' murmured Kim, as she sat beside her. 'Is that why you came? To see what I was doing?'

'Not at all,' her grandmother responded loftily. 'I told you, I was bored at home, and I thought—a few days in Vienna is just what I need. So I asked Mrs Smith to mind the dog, and took off. I must admit I was mildly *curious*, but that's all. And who is Jeanne?'

'I thought you'd never ask.' Kim stifled a yawn. 'Some woman who seems to be pursuing him. You may meet her—holy mackerel!' she clapped her hand to her mouth in sudden shock.

'What is it?'

'I hardly know how to tell you. But if anyone does come visiting while you're here, I'm well—er —Bryce and I are supposed to be engaged!'

'*What?*' It was Florence Dalby's turn for the look of startled horror, and maybe—just maybe, a touch of something else?

'Yes, it's a long story, but I'll tell you very quickly before I go to bed or you'll lie awake all night wondering, won't you?' Kim managed a cheeky grin at her grandmother, who sniffed.

'Huh! It seems as if I did right to come. One minute you're telling me something I had already surmised for myself—that you and Bryce strike sparks off each other—the next you're telling me that to all intents and purposes you are engaged. Am I mad or drunk, or what?'

'None. You see, it happened like this——' and Kim began with the ride out by car that had ended up with them all going for drinks to Jeanne's house. Her memory was faultless, her description vivid, and her grandmother listened in fascination, which grew as Kim gave her version of the final party on the previous Thursday which had culminated in Bryce's attack on Karl.

'Well, I'm quite speechless, my dear.' That was unusual. 'How absolutely devastating. Life is never dull, is it?'

'You could say that. But I'm falling asleep, love. It's a wonderful surprise to have you here, honestly.' Kim hugged her grandmother warmly. 'I'll see you in the morning. Goodnight.'

'Goodnight, my dear. Sleep well.' Florence Dalby closed the door after Kim. She looked very thoughtful.

Sunday morning. Distant church bells woke Kim and she lay listening to them, remembering her visit the previous day. She should have gone and looked inside. Perhaps one day she would... And then she thought: but it will have to be soon, for in another week or so I'll be going home, because, treasure or no, we will have covered the lake completely. Home. And then what? Join Jack in South America? More travel one way or another. And why, she thought, should the idea feel so hollow?

Kim was rarely depressed, and she was not going to allow herself to feel so now, when there was

144

Gran here, and they would be taking her to the lake later, to see if she was as good as she thought she was, always supposing the suit fitted her. It probably would, for Florence Dalby was slim like her granddaughter, and nearly as tall. Kim washed and dressed and went in to wake her. The room was empty.

Laughing voices came from the kitchen, and Kim made her way there, only half wondering, for she knew her grandmother too well...

Ann was rolling something that looked like pastry, and Florence Dalby was perched on a kitchen stool nearby, sipping coffee. ''Morning, darling,' she greeted Kim brightly. 'Ann and I are just having a little discussion on culinary matters. She's going to show me how she made that utterly delicious *apfelstrudel* we ate last night.'

'I thought you'd still be in bed,' Kim said. 'I should have known.'

'Breakfast won't be a minute, miss,' Ann stopped her rolling. 'Matt's just setting the places. Mr Drovnik and Mr Hillaby are down at the lake.'

'Oh, I see. Thanks, Ann.' Kim felt strangely restless. She didn't want to stay and talk, but she didn't want to leave either. The large airy kitchen was warm, with a spicy smell, and Kóshka sitting on a rug by an open fire licking his paws. She sighed and sat down, and Ann added:

'There's coffee in the pot if you'd like to help yourself.'

'Mmm, thanks.' She poured a cup of steaming hot coffee, and the back door opened and the two men came in. Kim's heart lifted. Bryce wore a dark

grey sweater and tight-fitting black trousers. He
was tall, smiling—handsome. The smile was not for
her, but for her grandmother.

'All is ready for you, madame,' he told her with a
grin. 'The boat is moved, all equipment prepared.
I think, if you will eat a light breakfast, we can go
soon, and then the rest of the day is yours.'

'Oh, Bryce, how wonderful! Really, I'm looking
forward to this no end, you just wouldn't believe.'

Gordon winked at Kim, who hid her smile. If
anyone had told her, a couple of weeks ago, where
she would be at this moment, and who with, she
would not have believed them. In a way, her life
had changed, but she didn't know why. There was
a clarity to everything, a sharpness she had never
noticed before, and she looked at Bryce, who was
deep in conversation with Ann and her grandmother about—of all things—*apfelstrudel*. It was
him. Bryce had made it so—but why? And how?
Kim did not know. She finished her coffee. In a
strange way she felt as if she were being carried
along on a current, on a tide which she was helpless
to resist. The sensation was an odd one, but at the
same time not unpleasant. And it was that last fact
that disturbed her.

They stood in the boat, Kim and Gordon, and
watched the two people in the water. 'She's a
bonny swimmer,' he conceded. 'I should have
known.'

'You should see her playing tennis,' said Kim,
laughing. 'I don't know where she gets her energy
from.' She saw the two heads bobbing in the lake,

quite a distance from them. Both wore snorkels, and were doing surface swimming. Bryce looked up and waved briefly, and then down again, so that only the back of his head could be seen, black and wet.

'Gordon,' asked Kim, for a certain question had been on her mind ever since their talk, 'what does Bryce do when he goes to this children's home?'

'Och, I don't know, I'm sure. I've never been with him and he rarely talks about it, only briefly, but I get the impression that he makes sure everything's running smoothly——' he stopped.

'And?' she prompted.

He shrugged. 'I think he's lonely. He has no family of his own at all, not a relative in the world. I think, when he goes there, it's like seeing himself when he was young. And he just wants to help them, that's all.' He shook his head. 'Do you not see why he gets on so well with your grandmother?'

It was like a sudden pain in Kim's heart. She closed her eyes for a moment. 'I think I do,' she answered quietly. She had never imagined she could feel sorry for someone so uncompromisingly tough as Bryce Drovnik, but strangely, just for a second, she did. She wanted to change the subject.

'I wonder when we'll find the plane?'

He gave her an odd look. Gordon was very shrewd. 'Could be tomorrow—the day after—who knows? That's where the excitement lies, in the uncertainty.'

'Like life,' murmured Kim, but so quietly that he didn't hear.

And then they were returning, and Kim prepared the beakers for their coffee, and the subject was abandoned. But not forgotten. Kim knew she could never forget Gordon's words.

Bryce took them all out in the Mercedes after lunch and they stopped for coffee in a café at the side of a road high in the hills. The view from there was spectacular. Distant snow-capped peaks soared into a flawless sky, darkening rapidly, becoming starlit even as they watched from their window table. They ate rich flaky pastry filled with spices and fruit, and they drank dark coffee from thick beakers, and Kim wondered if she had ever felt so happy and sad at the same moment. She poured thick yellow cream into her beaker, then looked up and her eyes met Bryce's across the table —and he smiled. And it seemed to Kim, in her strange mood, as if the smile held knowledge, as if of a secret shared—and then it was gone. Kim felt herself go cold. Had her grandmother said something to him about the Hungarian? It's my imagination, thought Kim. It's working overtime again. But suppose—just suppose—he had commented lightly to her on Kim's knowledge of Russian, and suppose Florence Dalby had said something like, 'Oh, yes, Kim learned that from a boy-friend— Hungarian, I think——' Kim picked up her beaker with steady hands. What did it matter? Memories of Laszlo had always been accompanied by a pang of regret—until this moment. Now she could see his face clearly in her mind's eye, and she felt nothing. Absolutely nothing. She was free of him at last. The coffee tasted suddenly very good.

'It's my treat,' her grandmother was saying. 'No, I absolutely *insist*. It's the very least I can do——' Kim scarcely heard. She was looking out through the window, leaving them to their amiable argument, looking out across the starlit mountains to where an infinity of sky stretched away for ever and ever. Space, she thought, men on the moon, and little green creatures in flying saucers, and I feel very remote all of a sudden as if I'm floating away ... And she turned then, to look at Bryce Drovnik, to see his profile sharply etched against a light behind him as he spoke to Gordon and her grandmother. And she knew why she felt so strange. She knew it as she watched his dark mobile features, the sudden laughter that occasionally lit his face, the eyes that could be so cold—and sometimes not cold. I don't hate him at all, she thought. I wonder why I ever imagined I did? I don't particularly like him either—but that might not be the point. He disturbs me and makes me restless in a way no one has done before. I don't think I'm falling in love with him because I can't love a man I don't like, can I? But at the same time—at the same time— the memory of his touch, and his kiss, comes back to me very strongly, and I can't ignore that fact any more. Kim cupped her chin in her hand and sighed. I must be mad, she thought. I'm all mixed up.

'You are far away again.' Bryce's voice was almost an intrusion into her thoughts. She looked up at him.

'Yes. I'm thinking.' Then she looked round and realised they were alone. Her grandmother and

Gordon were walking towards the door, talking and laughing animatedly. The warm café was deserted, save for them. Kim stood up, not wanting to be alone with him, because she felt tongue-tied, and that would never do. 'We'd better go,' she said. 'I enjoyed the coffee very much.'

'It was your grandmother's treat. She is a fine woman.'

'I know.' Kim smiled, then remembered Gordon's words. She picked up her handbag, and moved away from Bryce. Her heart had started to beat faster.

The only difference with their search on Monday morning was that Florence Dalby accompanied them, and waited with Gordon on board the boat. She had already decided to leave for home the following day, and had told them so, remaining adamant when Bryce told her that she was welcome to remain for as long as she cared to. Kim thought about that as she swam underwater. Trust Gran not to outstay her welcome. She had a fine sense of timing, and although Kim would be sorry to see her go, she knew as well as her grandmother that short visits are sweeter. The only difference with this one being that it would be the first and last. No continuing relationship this; Kim knew that quite well. They might have news of Bryce from Gordon in his spasmodic letters, but that would be all. Bryce Drovnik's world was not theirs, and although he had, albeit reluctantly, accepted Kim's presence for the duration of the hunt, she knew that when they said goodbye it would be final. For he didn't like her—he made that only too clear.

They did not dive again that afternoon. Bryce took them to visit the church, as it was her grandmother's last day, and Kim had told her of her own visit on the Saturday. The men waited in the car, and Kim and Florence Dalby wandered around the little church with its white walls and high dark-beamed ceiling. There was no one else there save an old woman polishing the wooden pews, who greeted them courteously in German.

As they went out again, Kim's grandmother said: 'So, my dear, I'm going home tomorrow, and I'll be sorry to go, but I made up my mind to just a few days when I set out.'

'I know, love. It's been super seeing you. I'll be home myself in a week or so.'

'Ah yes, so you will. Hmm.'

'What does that "hmm" mean, pra tell me?'

'Nothing, child, nothing at all. Come along, we mustn't keep the men waiting, must we? What a splendid host Bryce makes!' She linked her arm in Kim's and they made their way slowly back to the car. As they reached it, Florence Dalby looked back to the grave of her son, with its fresh flowers nodding brightly in the sunlight. Then they stepped into the Mercedes. Only the brightness of her eyes betrayed her.

'Today is the first day of the rest of my life.' The quotation came to Kim as she stood at her dressing table that evening. She didn't know why it should. She had read it once somewhere, and it had stuck in her mind, and now, as she carefully put the ring on to her finger, it came back again, as strongly as if she could see it written. They had eaten, and had been about to go into the lounge when Matthew had come in to say that Jeanne and Leo Wolfe were in the hall. They were passing, and had 'dropped in'.

The signal from Bryce to Kim, after the introductions to her grandmother had been smoothly performed, was imperceptible but plain—to her, She had excused herself and followed him out.

'I will bring the ring to your room in one minute,' he had said quietly.

And now she was here. A last flick of the comb and she was ready. As Bryce had handed the ring to her, Kim had said: 'I told my grandmother about our supposed engagement. Don't worry, she won't put her foot in it.'

He had grinned—very briefly. 'Good. I was hurrying down in case, but now——' a faint shrug '—I am sure she will entertain them well in my absence.'

'Yes. But perhaps you'd better go anyway. I want to make up—the competition, you know.' And she had given him a brittle smile as she held the door open.

Kim held up the hand with the ring on it to the light and repeated the quotation very softly under her breath. It seemed very appropriate. Just how she could not possibly foresee.

For a couple who had just 'dropped in', she thought as she sat listening to the ebb and flow of conversation around her, Jeanne and Leo seemed remarkably disposed to stay. Bryce was doing his best to keep the talk general, but Jeanne had annexed Florence Dalby, seemingly fascinated by her, and the two women were deep in conversation. Kim felt a faint twinge of unease. What if her grandmother slipped up? She didn't know the *whole* story—and then Kim mentally shrugged. What did it matter? What did anything matter? In a couple of weeks it would all be over anyway . . .

And then, at last, they were leaving, and the evening was over. In the hall Jeanne turned to Kim. Her dark eyes fathomless, her beautiful face held only the slightest of expressions as she said farewell to Kim, and then added softly: 'I did *so* enjoy meeting your grandmother. We had such a very interesting talk.' And then she smiled—slowly, and went out into the dark night, following her husband and Bryce. And Kim knew what that expression on her face had been. Jeanne *knew*. She knew the truth about their little masquerade.

CHAPTER TEN

THE morning of departure dawned, and Bryce was taking Florence Dalby to Vienna by helicopter to catch her plane. Kim hugged her as they stood outside the house. 'Phone when you get safely home,' she said. 'Promise now.'

'Of course I will. I have enjoyed this visit. It's been a wonderful weekend, really wonderful.' It was no use asking her what she and Jeanne had spoken about. No doubt Jeanne had thrown in some very casual question that her grandmother wouldn't even remember, had put two and two together in some devious way of her own—and that had been that. No one else had noticed, that was certain—and what point was there in saying anything? Kim kept her counsel. The sooner they found the treasure and ended the pointless masquerade, the better.

She watched Bryce help her grandmother into the helicopter, she and Gordon stood back, safely away from the lethal rotor blades, and waved as it rose clumsily into the air, then swooped away like a graceful bird.

'Aye, well, that's that,' said Gordon. 'Come on, lassie, let's away and have a cup of coffee.' And they went into the house to await Bryce's return.

Before they began diving that afternoon Bryce, Gordon, and Kim studied their map of the lake. The crossed-off portions were many now, and they were approaching the deeper centre of the Schwartzsee, which meant more care and skill were needed. They sat in the compact cabin of the boat as it rocked gently at anchor, and Bryce said:

'Ready, Kim?'

She nodded. 'Yes. Are you?'

'Yes. Then let us go.' He stood up, tall and straight. 'Coffee in two hours, Gordon.'

'Aye, aye, skipper.' Gordon cracked a smart salute, and Bryce grinned. That's what he is, Kim thought; the skipper—the captain. We might joke about it, but he's in charge, no doubt about that. I wonder if he'd be dismayed if he knew about Jeanne? Somehow she didn't think so. She could not imagine anything really bothering him. Anything—or anyone. She stood up and followed him up on deck. The hands that helped her on with her air tank were completely impersonal.

'Is that all right?' he asked her.

'Yes, thank you.' Gordon helped Bryce, then it was masks on, a final check that everything was working, flippers secured, and the backward dive over the side. A well established routine now, and they worked as a good team, and Kim knew the rules as well as Bryce, so why then did she feel suddenly unsure of herself, as if she were a beginner? It was ridiculous, but it was so.

They dived deeply, and she followed Bryce, keeping close, trying to quell an unreasoning panic inside her, almost a fear. That was it. She was tense and nervous, and it was dark, so very dark, even though Bryce carried a torch that beamed out, lighting the black places with an eerie glow, distorting the shadows so that they leaped and danced with a life of their own ... I want to go up, she thought, and swallowed in panic. I don't want to stay here, not with him——

She saw the beam swing round and strike her. It was as if he was a mind-reader. He swam back to her and took her arm and shook it urgently. It said as clearly as words could: 'What is the matter?'

She shook her head. She didn't know herself. She could not—must not—fail now. What would he think? She wrenched her arm free and signalled him to go on, but he stayed where he was, treading water, watching her. Then he pointed for Kim to go first so that he could follow, and she did so. But the sensation persisted. She felt as if she would *suffocate* if she stayed there a moment longer, and suddenly, hardly aware that she was doing so, started kicking upwards, upwards, upwards . . .

She was caught and held firmly by a pair of fantastically strong arms—and now she wanted to scream—but could not. You can't scream underwater, not at that depth, not without drowning—drowning—the light had gone out. They were in almost pitch darkness, fighting a silent battle, Kim struggling to release herself from a grip of steel, Bryce continuing to hold her, his arms round her body, his whole being concentrating in keeping her there, down. He was going to kill her . . . Kim lashed out with her legs, bent her elbow to dig into his chest, arched her body in one last desperate protest, and saw his arm come up towards her face —then knew no more.

She was lying on the deck, and the face that swam muzzily into view was Gordon's. He was strangely pale, and she heard his voice, as if from far away, say: 'She's round now.' Then Bryce was there, kneeling beside her, his wet suit shiny with water. 'Thank God,' he said, and she would have sworn he sounded relieved. 'Drink this,' he ordered, and she shook her head faintly as he pressed a flask to her lips.

'No——'

'*Drink it.*' The voice brooked no refusal. Kim sipped and spluttered, but felt immediately warmer, as fiery liquid went down into her stomach. She struggled to sit up and his hand was behind her, assisting her.

'Do you know what happened?' he said, and she shook her head.

'No. I panicked—I'm sorry. If I go down again now I'll be all right, I promise——'

'There was something wrong with the air, a fault in the line. I had to hit you. I am sorry, Kim, but I had to knock you out——'

She knew that her jaw was aching, and now she knew why. With a careful hand she reached up and touched her chin. And then she winced.

'W-why?' She wanted to cry all of a sudden.

'You were struggling to get to the surface. We were too deep. You could have been killed. I had to bring you up slowly—that was the only way to do it. I had to leave the torch behind.' So that was why it had gone black all of a sudden.

She leaned forward and Bryce said: 'Come, let us go down to the cabin. Give me your hand.' Then he bent and lifted her, and she was swung up into his arms as though she were a baby. He carried her down to the cabin and she smelt coffee as Gordon came out of the galley bearing a steaming beaker.

'Here, get this down you, lassie,' he said. He was grinning all over his face now, the anxiety gone. Kim even managed to grin back at him.

'Thanks, Gordon.' Bryce went out, running up the steps and on to the deck, and Gordon sat opposite Kim at the table.

'Och, you had me worried then, lassie, I'll not

mind admitting it now. To see the two of you bobbing to the surface, you as limp as a rag doll—och!' he shook his head. It was a sobering thought.

Kim bit her lip. 'I thought it was me. I thought I was panicking for no reason.'

'Not you. You're a professional, same as him. He's checking the air now. He'll find out exactly what it is.'

'I must go down again.' She stood up, still a little shaky, and he held her arm.

'Are you sure?'

'Yes. You know as well as I do. It's like falling off a horse—or being thrown. If you're not to lose your nerve you have to get on again as quickly as possible. Come on, we'll tell him.'

Bryce was busy on deck, and looked up from the air line as Kim approached him. 'How soon can we dive again?' she asked him.

'You are better?'

'Yes.'

'Are you sure?'

'Yes.' Bryce looked at the watch he wore on his wrist. 'Then we will go down again in fifteen minutes. There was an air-lock in your breathing tube. It is all right now, but we will exchange and you will use mine.'

'All right.' She looked at him as he slowly straightened up from the deck. 'You saved my life,' she said.

'I only did what I had to. You would have done the same.'

She gave a wry smile. 'I can't see me managing to knock you out.' She saw the quick flash of his white teeth, heard the laughter that followed.

'No? I can teach you some quick techniques that will do the trick.'

'Not now. Some other time, perhaps.' She turned away and put her hands on the railing and looked out over the dark sombre water. She still felt rather weak, not surprisingly, but her determination to go down again was as strong as ever. She sensed him moving towards her, and then his voice came softly from beside her.

'Do not worry. We will take it gently this time. I shall watch you all the time. We will swim side by side—just for half an hour. That will be enough.'

'You're in charge. Anything you say.' She looked up at him. He was too near. Much too near.

'You will have a bruise on your jaw for a few days.'

'It's a small price to pay,' she answered. 'When my grandmother phones—I would rather she didn't know.'

'Of course not. Come, let us get ready.' He touched her arm lightly. 'We must find the torch. That is our first task.'

They double-checked everything this time, and then were going down into the depths, with a spare torch to help them search for the first one, and after a few moments Kim lost her first fear. Then she knew she had done the right thing.

The expected telephone call came that evening from Kim's grandmother. They all spoke to her, and when the call was over, Kim excused herself and went to bed. She was tired, and her jaw hurt, although she would not admit it even to herself, because she wanted to be fit for the next morning's dive. She slept soundly and was much better by the time she awoke the following morning. It was Wednesday. She wondered if they would have any luck. They didn't. Thursday was the same, and she wondered if they were on a wild goose chase, if it would be better to call the whole thing off.

Friday was a dark day, and the full sullen skies exploded with snow that morning, so that they decided to leave the diving until it cleared. Kim stood at the lounge window after a light lunch and looked at the white expanse of garden. How quickly everything had changed from autumn to winter. A watery sun struggled to free itself from dark cotton wool clouds, and she thought that the weather was hardly conducive to success. And yet at the same time a small restless urge was building up inside her, and it would not go away. She wondered what it was, and turned as she heard someone come into the room. It was Bryce.

'Are we going down this afternoon?' she asked him.

'Do you want to?' he seemed almost amused.

'Yes. I have the strangest feeling——' she shrugged, waiting for his cynical smile, but it didn't come.

'What you choose to call a woman's intuition?'

'If you like.' She shivered, suddenly strangely cool.

'Then we will go. I was thinking anyway that it was clearing up. Yes, we will tell Gordon. He is on the telephone to someone in Vienna at the moment. When he is finished, we will dive. Do you wish to change now?'

'Yes, I'd better.' She moved to pass him and he touched her chin lightly.

'The bruise is out now. You put that ointment on that I gave you?'

'Yes, thank you.' She was breathless again, as she always was when he was too near. 'Excuse me.'

'Of course.' He stood aside to let her pass. And he watched her.

The snow wasn't deep, but it was crisp—as crisp as the cold air they breathed on their way to the lake. Kim looked at the boat. The feeling still persisted. A tingle of excitement that refused to go away. She had never felt like this before; and it was almost unnerving—quite heady, as though she had drunk too much champagne.

Then they were going down, in a new part of the lake, not quite as deep, but they needed their torches because it was darker. It was also colder, but they swam more vigorously and the lack of heat was soon forgotten. The two hours had nearly passed with no result, and Kim looked at her watch as Bryce signalled her, and she gave him the thumbs-up sign. They were moving—and she swung the beam round almost carelessly, just for one last look—and she saw the dark shadowy hulk. Then she knew.

Her grip on his arm was powerful with a strength she didn't know she possessed—and he turned slowly. Turned and saw—then looked at Kim. Heart beating fast, she followed him to the black shapeless mass of tangled metal that lay half buried by sand, watched him uncoil the length of wire from his belt and attach it firmly to a thrusting shard of steel. It was frightening. They had searched fruitlessly for so many days and now suddenly the search was over, and she didn't want to see any more. She just wanted to be back at the house. It was as if everything was happening in a dream, slow motion, shadowy, disturbing.

The wire curled and snaked upwards to take a tiny marker buoy to the surface, ready for them to find the exact spot again. And they followed it. Bryce would do nothing now. Their time was up for the day, and there must be no mistakes. Kim's intuition had been right—and following it now came a sense of foreboding that she took with her on the slow ascent to the surface. There was no feeling of achievement or triumph, nothing save the helpless inexorable sensation of things being taken out of her hands.

Gordon had seen the bright red flash of the marker buoy before they surfaced. He was standing at the rail, laughing, and he gave them the raised arms gesture of success as they swam towards him.

'I don't believe it!' he shouted, and leaned over to haul Kim aboard. 'I don't *believe* it!' She was shivering, but it wasn't with the excitement. She felt very cold all of a sudden, and somehow sad. But she didn't know why. Bryce helped her off with the air tank, and then his own, and then he clapped Gordon on the back.

'We did it!' he said, dark green eyes gleaming, 'or should I say Kim did. She found the wreck just as we were about to finish for the day.' Gordon hugged her. 'Well done, love.' Then, more hesitantly: 'Why, what is it, lassie? You're quite pale.'

'I'll be all right in a minute. I'm cold, that's all.'

'Why, you're shivering! Down in the cabin with you. I'll put the heater on and bring you your coffee. You'll be fine in a moment.'

'Yes, of course I will.' Bryce was watching her too. She turned and left them, aware that they exchanged a glance, sensing their puzzlement, but uncaring.

It was early evening, and she and Bryce were alone in the house. Kim sat by the fire with Kóshka on her knee and tried to relax as she went over the events of the afternoon in her mind. Everything seemed to be happening at once in a dizzying spiral. Gordon had gone to Vienna in the helicopter, taking Ann and Matthew for an unexpected weekend off. It had been decided by Bryce and him on their return to the house. She could understand why in a way. Everything was still a secret, and there would be much activity over the next couple of days. Kim leaned her head back wearily. Gordon would return later that night after attending to some business in Vienna, and in the morning—in the morning—she closed her eyes. Soon it would all be over and she would go back to England, and never see Bryce again. Never.

'You wish for a drink, Kim?' his voice interrupted her thoughts and she sat up guiltily.

'No, thank you. What time will Gordon be back?'

'About eleven, I think. We will eat soon. Ann

has left our meal ready in the oven.'

'Yes, I know.' She felt stifled. She didn't want to be alone with him. 'I'll go and get washed—excuse me.' She put the cat gently down and stood up.

'Are you not pleased?' he asked softly. Kim looked at him.

'Yes—yes, of course.' But she couldn't add anything. She couldn't say what was wrong with her because she didn't know. Quickly, quietly she went out of the room and upstairs. It had started to snow again, gently, softly, and she stood at the window and watched the swirling white flakes blurring the sky, the mountains, the trees. A car's engine grew louder and then stopped. It couldn't be Gordon, because he was in the helicopter, so who——?

The bell rang a shrill imperious summons that echoed through the night, filling the quiet house, and she turned away from the window and went to the door and waited. There were voices. Bryce's and Jeanne's. Low and urgent, her voice, then it faded as the two went into the lounge. She had come alone. But why? It's nothing to do with me, thought Kim, and went into the bathroom to wash her face.

She couldn't stay up there for ever. She would have to go down some time. And what was Jeanne saying? That she knew of their stupid masquerade? And how would she look when Kim entered the room? Amused—angry—contemptuous? She tilted her chin. Let her look how she wanted, it was Bryce's problem, not hers. Kim was weary of the whole business. She ran a brush through her defiant curls and went down the stairs. I don't *care*, she told herself.

It helped her to repeat it as she opened the lounge door silently. I don't care—I don't—then she froze, her thoughts scattering in shock at what she saw before her. Jeanne and Bryce kissing each other, the woman's arms tight round his neck, his on her waist or arms, Kim could not see clearly because her eyes were blurred. Engrossed in each other, heedless—until Kim turned and went out, closing the door behind her. She heard their voices as she ran upstairs, heard Jeanne's deep rich laugh ring out.

She sank on the bed, hand to mouth, her whole body trembling with shock. And with realisation of the truth that had been staring her in the face for days, and which she had tried to ignore. Now she could do so no longer. The searing agony of jealousy was too strong to be borne, and Kim put her face in her hands, rocking gently back and forth in pain. She didn't hate Bryce Drovnik, she loved him, deeply and desperately.

CHAPTER ELEVEN

KIM thought that there could be nothing worse than the agony of the next minutes. In a kind of numbed trance, she heard their voices, heard the front door close, then Bryce:

'Kim? Where are you?'

She took a deep, shuddering breath. Now. Now

was the time. She must appear calm. He must not know; must never know. It was a supreme effort, but she managed it, summoning all her will power to her aid.

'I'll be down in a minute,' she called. She had done it. She had sounded quite composed. He would know she had been down. Far better to explain before he had a chance to ask.

He was in the kitchen, at the stove, and half turned as she went in.

'I'm sorry,' she said, 'if I came down at the wrong moment. So I went up again,' and she smiled. 'Is the dinner ready? Good. I'm quite hungry.'

'Yes. We'll eat it here if you have no objection.'

'What a good idea. It saves work, doesn't it?' She knew she was being terribly bright and cheerful, but she couldn't help it. It was her only defence against the awful pain that filled her. And if Bryce saw, he said nothing. He was quieter than usual, and he looked at her as she fetched plates and cutlery, but she could not read anything in his expression. It was quite unfathomable. I love you, she thought, but I don't know you. You are infinitely strong and powerful, and I have no defence against my feelings, but at least I can hide them from you —if I try hard enough.

She was determined to eat. Let him see her picking at her food and he might guess. She would finish it if it choked her. It nearly did—but she managed it, even though she felt sick. She even managed to say, when the meal was over—five minutes later she could not even remember what it had been—that she would make coffee for them both.

He nodded. 'Thank you. I have one or two phone calls to make, but I shall not be long.' He went out. Kim looked out of the window as she waited for the percolator to bubble. The snow had thickened. It swirled round and down in a thick dizzying mass of blurry white that had an almost hypnotic effect. But all she saw was a woman in a man's arms...

'It is not ready yet?'

'What!' She started in dismay, then realised that he was merely asking in a pleasant enough tone, and added: 'Oh, not quite. I'll bring it in.'

'I phoned to Gordon just now. There was something I had thought of that he could have brought back here with him for the final search of the plane tomorrow—and he said he was just about to call me.' And then he stopped. Kim looked at him, puzzled. There was something rather disturbing in his eyes. 'There is a snowstorm in Vienna, and it is getting worse. He will come back in the morning.'

'Oh, I see.' But she didn't, not really, not then. It was only minutes later, as she took the coffee through to the lounge, that the full impact struck her. She and Bryce were completely alone in the house, and would be all night.

She knew she would manage to get through the evening somehow. There was a good film on the television, and books to read—and if Bryce wanted to talk about the plane, why, she would even do that. Anything as long as he never guessed the truth about her. It would only be for a few more days anyway, and then she would leave.

She thought about that later on when Bryce had

gone out to feed the two alsatians, Boris and Valery. She had been a virtual prisoner at first—she had forgotten Bryce's attempt at moral blackmail. It had worked, oh, how it had worked! And Gordon had never guessed—and now it didn't seem to matter any more, because soon she could go away. She would be free. Free! she echoed to herself. How strange a freedom it will be now, because part of me will be left behind here at the house by the Schwartzsee. But I've had a bruised heart before. I'll get over it. It will pass. But would it? Kim lifted Kóshka on to her knee and began to stroke the slender black creature. She closed her eyes. She had imagined herself in love with Laszlo for a short time, but now she knew something she could not admit before. Her feelings towards him had been but a pale shadow compared to the rich deep texture of what she was experiencing now. She put her hand to her eyes, pressing hard as if to relieve some agonising pressure.

And Bryce loved Jeanne. He had pretended, for obscure reasons of his own, that he wanted to be rid of her, but it was not so. Perhaps the idea of the mock engagement suited him well enough—Kim recalled suddenly, and with pain, just how amused he had been when it had first been suggested—to serve to make Jeanne jealous, to bring her to heel. And it had worked, oh yes, it had worked all right. Very well indeed.

She looked at her watch as Bryce walked into the room. She didn't want to stay there any longer with him. It was only ten o'clock, but she had two good books to read.

'I am going for a walk with the dogs,' he told her. 'It is very deep and crisp, the snow, and they like that. Will you be all right on your own?'

'Of course. I was just going to bed anyway. If you don't mind?'

'Of course not.' His voice was deep. He looked at her, and she wondered what there was in his eyes—and his voice—that could so disturb her. 'I have my keys. No one can get in. In any case, I shall not be too long,' then he smiled as he turned to go out. He's going to meet *her*, Kim thought wildly. Of course, that's it! What a fool I am! She shivered, hating Jeanne, hating herself, hating *him*.

She heard the snap of the back door and waited, heard him whistle, and a responding bark, then all was silence again. Restless now, she went out and tried the handle, and the door was locked. The snow had eased considerably, and the sky could be seen, rich dark velvet with a pure white moon staring serenely down.

She shrugged, warmed up some coffee that remained in the pot, and carried it up to bed with her. She thought she could not possibly sleep, but she was more tired than she had imagined, and as the book grew heavier, and her eyelids drooped, she lay back, and, reaching up, switched off the overhead light.

A dog's bark woke her from a particularly vivid dream, and Kim sat up, bathed in perspiration. She had been swimming in the lake, and dark creatures peopled the waters, faceless, nameless *things* that threatened and frightened her. She waited for the heartbeats to slow down, and listened again in case the barking was repeated—or if it had only been part of the dream. Then she heard another, more distant sound; the banging of a door. It was the door to the boathouse. Fear prickled the hairs on the back of her neck. Something was wrong. Switching on the light, she saw that it was half past one. Bryce would be asleep—unless the noises had woken him up too—and she had to let him know.

Pulling on her housecoat, Kim padded along to his bedroom and tapped on the door, which swung slowly open to reveal an empty bed, neatly made up—untouched since morning. She took a deep breath; so he was still out. He hadn't returned, but the dogs, or at least one of them, had. He could be with Jeanne somewhere—or he could have had an accident, and there was only one way to find out. Feeling suddenly very lonely, Kim ran back along the corridor to her own room and pulled on her trews over her pyjamas, her coat over her pyjama top, and her flat walking shoes. There was a determination within her that effectively banished fear. She ran downstairs. The hall and kitchen lights were still on, as they had been all evening. Kóshka looked up sleepily from his basket in a corner, and yawned. He wasn't remotely concerned in anything.

Kim put the catch up on the door and closed it softly behind her. The snow was swirling about again and it caught in her eyelashes in soft furry lumps, making her blink and put up her hand to brush the flakes away.

'Boris, Valery!' she called, and a black shape

bounded out of the white blur, tail wagging enthusiastically. She didn't know which one it was. 'Good dog,' she said. 'Where is he?' The only response to that was a deep-throated woof. Already her shoes were clogged with snow, her coat had changed to white, but nothing was going to stop her getting to the boathouse. The image of Bryce lying unconscious by the boat was too powerful to be ignored. 'Come on, boy,' she said. She would be safe with him. If it was not Bryce, but an intruder —perhaps someone trying to find the plane—he would protect her. She shivered, suddenly conscious of the contrast from warm bedroom to this. The mountains could not be seen at all. Even the trees that screened the lake were a blurred grey, and Kim had to keep blinking and brushing her face to see at all. Boris—or was it Valery?—didn't seem to mind. He bounded ahead of her with almost puppylike enthusiasm, stopping only to sniff at the snow and emerge white-nosed before running off. It was eerie going through the trees, for here there was little snow, and that mainly caught in the branches, but the reflection from that outside filtered in in a strange shadowy half light, and Kim called the dog to her sharply. She was not afraid, but...

He walked docilely now, just in front of her, padding silently, obedient to her command. 'Good boy,' she whispered. 'Good boy,' and he wagged his tail a little, as if he understood the words.

She saw the boathouse as they emerged from the trees, and her heart lurched. What if—what if he were there—*with her*? But there was no car, at least she had seen none—Kim closed her eyes. She could not go back now, she had to look, but at least she would call out first.

'Bryce,' she said softly, then, a little louder: 'Bryce, are you there?'

No answer. Nothing. There was no light, no sound, no movement. The dark waters of the lake were still, swallowing the snowflakes as they touched its surface, leaving no trace.

'Come on, boy, let's have a look.' And as she went nearer the door swung slowly open, creaking, and stayed ajar, caught by the soft snow, caught in a gentle trap. She opened the door wider. The boat was there, in darkness, and that was all. No Bryce, either unconscious or with Jeanne, no second dog, not even a mouse. Kim took a deep breath and let it out slowly. That was that. Back to the house as quickly as possible and lock up again—it was all she could do. She patted the alsatian's head. 'Come on, boy,' she said. 'We'll go back now.' She closed the door this time, and locked it. That would not bang again anyway.

But where was he? Nearly two o'clock, and he had said he would not be long. It was absurd to be worrying. She shouldn't care at all. Bryce was the sort of man who could look after himself in any situation—he had proved that, more than once. He was hard, tough, powerful, resourceful—and aggressive. And I love him, she thought. I love him in a way that hurts, and that's why I care. He might be back at the house now. He could have returned —of course! she thought. He'll be there now—he will be there.

She could not go too fast because walking was difficult, her shoes felt like leaden weights, and it was uphill anyway—and cold. She pulled the coat more tightly round her and tucked in a stray, snow-sodden wisp of hair under her furry hood. She would soon be in the trees and then she could scrape off the surplus snow from her shoes, brush her coat down, and try and run to the house ... The blanket of snow effectively covered the ground, hiding unevennesses that would be perfectly obvious at other times, covering rocks as well, so well that they were completely invisible, just appearing as slight bumps in that smooth unbroken surface. So that Kim saw nothing, felt nothing, until suddenly and surprisingly, the ground was rushing up to meet her and she had scarcely time to put her hands out in an instinctive gesture of self-protection before she found herself whirling round in a dizzying spiral of stars and snow. Stars and snow. And then—darkness. Complete and all-enveloping and warm.

She was back in the same dream again; the one where she was in the lake, with weird monsters—and the dream had been shattered by a dog's bark, as it was again. She opened her eyes. But she wasn't in bed, as she had been before, she was very cold, and covered in white fur—white *fur*! Kim put her hand up to her face and the fur crumpled into fine powder and vanished. Snow. She lay there for a moment, considering it, and the dog's bark came again, nearer, excited—and now it wasn't just one dog but two. It was absurd. She was here, in the snow, and she had no idea—then she remembered that she had come out with Boris—or Valery, it seemed vastly unimportant which—to find Bryce. That was it! Bryce. But she hadn't, and now she knew she was going to lie there until she froze unless she did something about it. Her head ached. She knew that all right. Tentatively she tried moving first her legs, then her other arm. So far, so good. But why were the dogs——?

'Kim, I have found you—oh, Kim!' But that was Bryce's voice. Bryce—but he had vanished. It was getting too much, really too much. She couldn't see him—of course not, it was all her imagination anyway. She struggled to sit up, before lethargy overcame her—and felt his arms round her, helping her, and then she looked up, because those hands were too real to be a hallucination, and saw Bryce's face swim into view. Then, quite ridiculously, she fainted.

She was in her bedroom when she opened her eyes again. But not alone. Bryce was there with her, the last remnants of the snow in his raven black hair melting fast in the warmth, leaving only glittering drops of moisture that melted away, away . . . Kim watched, fascinated, too numb to do otherwise, for she was still dazed with her fall, and her arms and legs felt heavy. She was propped up on her bed, and he was saying: 'No, your right arm first. So. That is it.' He was helping her off with her coat. When he had eased it from her he put it over the radiator by the window. Kim sat and watched him. Her mind was starting to function again, slowly.

'I went to look for you,' she said, as he came towards her carrying a fluffy pink towel from the bathroom. 'I heard the boathouse door slam—and I thought—I thought——' she knew she was speaking slowly, but she couldn't help it, 'you'd been hurt, so I went down with one of the dogs, I don't know which one——'

'Boris,' he interrupted gently. 'It was Boris. Ah! So that explains it. But why did you think I was out there?' He began to rub her hair and face, quite carefully with the towel. 'You are soaking wet. You must get dry soon or you will be ill.'

'Because you weren't in your bed——'

'But I was in my study working out certain things for tomorrow. Ah, that you did not think to look there—I am so sorry——'

He hadn't been out after all! Her teeth began to chatter with delayed shock. She had gone out... 'What happened to me?' she asked. Her head tingled with his touch, and it was exceedingly difficult to think coherently, but she must try, she must not let him see.

'You tripped over a hidden stone and tumbled over. I think perhaps you hit your head and knocked yourself out. The dog's barking disturbed me. Valery must have been somewhere else on his own, but Boris was going frantic scratching at the back door. I went, of course, to see why, and he barked and barked until at last I followed him— and found you.' He sighed and paused in his task, so that his hands rested on Kim's shoulders. He looked down at her. 'You were struggling to sit up when I called you. Then you fainted and I carried you back here.'

She wanted him to go away. She wanted him to go away *now*. She could hardly breathe with the nearness of him, the overwhelming strength and power of him filling her with treacherous dizzying weakness.

'Please——' she began. 'Please—I'll be all right now. I can—manage on my own.' And she began to stand up—or rather, she tried to, then he helped her to her feet, and it was all so easy because he was very strong, and his arms, instead of moving away, were moving around her, so that she was held. Kim's heart beat so fast she thought she would suffocate.

'Please——' she began again. A ridiculous word, she always seemed to be saying it, but it was all she could think of. And then he kissed her.

Bryce kissed Kim, kissed Kim—it was an endless kiss that went on and on, and after the first startled surprise she found herself responding, putting her arms up, sliding them around the back of his neck. His damp hair tickled her fingers, his neck was so strong—and she realised just precisely what she was doing. Horrified, filled with sudden shame, she pushed him away.

'Oh! How can——'

'Do not push me away.' His voice was deeper, quieter, more husky, and he moved in, his arms securing her more firmly, his intention obvious. But it was too late. For Jeanne's face was there, filled with mocking laughter, the way she had looked at Kim when she *knew*. And he had kissed Jeanne tonight, Kim had seen them, and been stricken with jealousy. Perhaps he didn't care. Perhaps, if he could not get the woman he wanted, Kim would be a substitute.

'No. Oh no, you *don't*!' she gasped. 'Not me. Not *me*! Leave me alone!' And this time she found her strength. She used the palm of her hand to push upwards, hard, at his chin, which had the desired effect of jerking his head back. 'Get out of my room!' She was shaking, her voice was shaking, but there was no mistaking the vehemence of her words. 'You must think I'm stupid. Do you really think I'm that naïve?' She backed away from him. They were alone in the house. She had woken from a nightmare, struggled out into the snow, been knocked unconscious, and now, worst of all, seemed to be in the middle of a second, far more disturbing nightmare.

It was as if everything was happening in some kind of slow motion, as in a film, where in sudden flashback, time is altered so that every moment becomes precise and measured; timeless.

'I loathe you,' she said, and even the words seemed to echo in the stillness before they reached him, before she saw the dark green eyes darken further, become—what? Angry? 'I hate you.' And half turning, she picked up a small statuette from her bedside table and held it aloft. Smouldering resentment of his cavalier treatment exploded in one moment of white heat as the memory of Jeanne's mocking face mingled with images of *him*; his hardness, the moral blackmail; the brutal kisses; the scene with her handbag—all came to a point of fire as she held the little statue and shakingly said:

'Don't come near me——'

'You do not need to *defend* yourself.' His voice was harsh now. 'Not against *me*. Thank you for telling me what you think of me,' and he turned away from her, the panther, the dark silent enemy whose arms had held her, and he moved away from her towards the door. In a way it was symbolic; his walking away. Something had finished, been severed. His words as he reached the door confirmed that: 'I shall not touch you again,' he said. 'Goodnight.'

He had gone. Kim lowered the statuette on to the table. Her hand was trembling, and she put it to her face. Hot tears scalded the back of her eyes, but she was determined not to shed them. She found a clean pair of pyjamas, undressed, and put them on. She knew that she had to get away as soon as possible. The plane had been found; the reason for her coming had been justified, and she could no longer live in the same house as Bryce Drovnik, not even for just a few days. She crawled into bed, aching all over and hurting inside with the deeper pain that came from the knowledge of having been used. Bryce had wanted to make love to her. Not because he loved her, but simply because she had been there, and vulnerable. Kim buried her burning face in the cool sheets. Today, she thought. Today, one way or another, I will get away from here, and from this man. The resolve was made, and was irrevocable. And because that was so, she slept.

It all came back to her when she woke several

hours later to the unmistakable sound of the helicopter blades slowing, clicking to a stop. Gordon! Gordon was back! Kim's heart lifted. Everything would be all right now. He would understand. He would find a way.

She dressed in warm red sweater and dark trews. Her coat over the radiator was now bone dry, no trace of snow—and warm. She left it there and went downstairs.

She needed to speak privately to Gordon, and had assumed she would have to wait her opportunity, but the house was silent and empty, and a piece of paper on the table caught her eye as she went into the kitchen. She had never seen Bryce's writing before, only the scribbled bits on maps. But this was a note, clearly for her. 'I have gone to the village. Back at ten.' That was all it said. The writing was bold and dark and upright—just like him, she thought wryly. She put the paper down, and as she went to the back door to open it for Gordon she knew precisely what she was going to do now.

'But I *cannot* do it. At least wait until he returns.' Gordon looked so worried that Kim would have hated herself at any other time. But now the desire, amounting almost to an obsession to get away, was paramount, and it was all she could think of. Nothing else mattered. It was nearly nine-thirty. She had made then both coffee and Gordon sat drinking his while Kim stood, too agitated to do likewise.

'Please, Gordon. *Please*. I'll never ask you another favour as long as I live. I'll be forever in your

179

debt.'

'But why? What has the man done, for heaven's sake? He's not——' he stopped, eyes on her, and she shook her head.

'I can't tell you. No, not *that*,' but near enough, she added inwardly, only I'll never tell anyone, ever. 'But I can't stay. I *hate* him, I'm not stopping here a minute longer and if you won't take me I'll set off walking to the station right now. I'll find it, even if it takes me hours. I've got a good idea where it is. I'm going, and that's all there is to it. I'm sorry, Gordon, that it had to end like this, but——' and suddenly to her own complete astonishment and dismay, Kim burst into tears.

'Och, lassie. There, there.' He came round to her, his kindly face filled with deep concern, and put his arms round her. 'It must be something bad to do this to you. Aye well, ye've won. I'll take you. Best hurry now.'

She smeared the tears away with a shaky hand. 'Yes, I will. It'll not take me a moment to pack. Wait there.' She sped away upstairs, and within five minutes was back with one case. 'Can you send the other on?' she asked him. 'I've left it in my room.' She took a deep shaky breath. 'Please—let's go, Gordon.'

He took the case from her. 'Come on away then, Kim.'

She knelt to stroke the black cat. 'Goodbye, Kóshka,' she said. The two dogs were at the door, as if they knew. She had become quite fond of them; giant fierce creatures that they were, there was a touch of gentleness in their natures too.

She patted them, and then, without a backward glance, walked towards the helicopter. A hard dry ache in her throat would not go away. She was running away, something for which she despised herself. She had never run away from anything—or anyone—before. But then she had never met a man like Bryce before. She would never see him again. Never. She knew that now. Something in her life was over.

CHAPTER TWELVE

'BUT, my dear child, of course I'm delighted to see you home again. I just didn't expect you back so *soon*, that's all.' Florence Dalby smiled warmly at Kim and passed her a hot toasted crumpet dripping with butter. I don't know what's the matter with me, thought Kim. It's as if I need reassurance that I've done the right thing. I feel as unsure of myself as a child.

It was early Saturday evening. The rain lashed down outside, a complete contrast to the snow she had left behind; and Rinty, her grandmother's faithful golden labrador, sprawled contentedly at Kim's feet, pausing from sleep only occasionally to lick her toes. The fire was hot, Kim was sleepy after the travelling that had been accomplished in such a hurried manner, and she wondered how soon she might decently go to bed. Then she might avoid the questions...

She might have been a mind-reader. 'It's quite all right,' her grandmother said softly, catching Kim's glance as it left the fire. 'You don't have to tell me anything you don't wish to. I can guess that something went wrong. That much would be obvious to a three-year-old—but, nosey as I may be, if you don't want to talk about it, I won't pry.' And she reached out and patted Kim's hand.

'Oh, Gran, I don't think I'd know where to begin.' Kim shook her head. 'It's just that—that I realised I was in love with—Bryce.' She swallowed hard. 'And he's most definitely not in love with me. That's putting it at its simplest.'

'Oh *dear*.' Florence Dalby sighed. 'Life can be difficult at times. I'm so sorry, my dear, truly sorry. But you're home now, that's the important thing— and you're tired too, I can see that. I'll go up and switch on the electric blanket and you can go to bed just as soon as you wish.'

'I think I'll go out and join Jack,' Kim said suddenly. 'I can go next week. I've had all the right injections. I wonder if he'll send me the fare if I wire him?'

'I think you need a few days' rest before you go tearing off again, love,' her grandmother said mildly.

'No, I don't. I'll be fine after a good night's sleep —honestly, you'll see. I'm as strong as a horse.'

'Hmm! Well, you know best. I've never been one to boss you about, as well you know—now,' briskly, 'let's see what's on television, shall we? And perhaps a little drink for us both later on.'

'Mmm, lovely, thanks, Gran. Did I ever tell you

you were wonderful?'

'Yes, but I can stand it being repeated. Now, put your feet up and I'll away and do your blanket.'

The phone rang shrilly in the hall just after her grandmother had gone up. Kim was about to go and answer it when it stopped and she heard her grandmother's voice faintly from her bedroom, where she had an extension. She relaxed in the chair, watching the picture as it emerged from the ether, a Western—and she wondered what Bryce was doing at that moment. She caught her breath. No, I mustn't, she thought. I'm going to start to forget him—and as soon as possible. She wondered how long that would take her.

Bedtime, and Kim kissed her grandmother fondly. 'If I'm up early enough in the morning, I might go to church,' she said.

'I'd go with you, love, but Mrs Hutchinson might call round,' her grandmother answered.

'Oh, was it she who phoned? I was going to answer it when I heard you on.'

'You did? Oh—yes, that's right. Well now, you run up and I'll bring you a glass of hot milk up—you'll sleep like a log.'

Kim grinned. 'I will anyway. But thanks. You spoil me.' But she wondered as she went upstairs if her imperturbable grandmother had actually, just for a moment, seemed slightly confused.

She slept so well that it was nearly nine when she woke up the following morning. Stretching, Kim went to the window and looked out. Another rainy autumn day. 'Umbrella and wellies,' she said, and shivered. When she was washed and dressed, she went downstairs, to a waiting breakfast of bacon and eggs. There was something different about Florence Dalby, and Kim looked at her. 'Are you all right?' she asked, pausing in the act of buttering toast.

'Me? All right? I'm fine—never felt better. Why do you ask?'

Kim shrugged. 'I don't know. It's just—something about you. Mmm, you're all made up for a start—and you've got some gorgeous perfume on. What is it?'

'Chamade. And you make it sound as if I'm an awful old frump who's just blossomed out——'

'Oh, Gran!' Kim laughed at the unlikely picture conjured up. 'You know I didn't mean that!'

'I know, love. I'm only joking. Eat up your breakfast. You don't want to be late, do you?'

Kim looked at her watch. 'No. Fifteen minutes' walk—oh, I'll be there by ten—and back at half past eleven.'

'Right then. I'll probably potter about when you've gone. Water the plants in the conservatory, that sort of thing.' She patted her hair and smiled at Kim. There *was* something odd—but Kim couldn't decide just what.

She set off walking, refusing the offer of a lift in her grandmother's Mini, because she genuinely enjoyed walking in the rain, She contrasted the houses and gardens, grey and dripping in the wet, with the place she had so recently left—and then chided herself. She was back now, home in Cheshire, even if only for a brief time, and Austria would

*—must—*soon be forgotten. Then one day it would be a memory to take out, perhaps even to enjoy. Perhaps ... She lifted her head high and walked briskly along the shiny pavements.

She opened the front door with her key and pushed it wide open. Rinty bounded out from the living room and greeted her with a woof and a tail wag. But there was no call of welcome. The house seemed strangely silent.

'Gran?' Kim called. Rinty whined and cocked his head to one side. But no one answered. It was very strange—everything was odd, but Kim didn't know why, only that now, quite suddenly, her heart was beginning to beat faster. She repeated the word as she walked towards the living room. She had maybe fallen asleep—only it was something she never did. The door was ajar. Rinty pushed past her as if to say: Look who's here—and Kim walked in. Because now she knew why the house was so silent, why her grandmother wasn't there, and she looked the length of the room to see the man standing by the window, and she said, quite quietly: 'Why have you come?'

'Because you left my house.' Bryce walked slowly towards her. He was dressed very conservatively in a charcoal grey suit, white shirt, dark tie. He looked big, handsome, unsmiling—and somehow tired, as if he had journeyed long and far with little sleep.

Kim knew her legs wouldn't support her for much longer. He stood before her, a couple of feet away—very still. 'Where is my grandmother?' she asked.

'She went out.'

'It was——' she realised something she should have known before, knew why she had seen confusion on her grandmother's face the previous night. 'It was you who phoned, wasn't it?' she asked quietly.

'Yes, it was. We had a—talk. Your grandmother invited me to come today.'

'Oh.' Kim let out her breath in a long deep sigh. 'She shouldn't——'

'I was already here—in England. I was phoning from Manchester Airport. If she had told me to stay away I would still have come. I would have waited outside until I saw you. But she didn't. She invited me to come here. She said that you intend to go to South America in a few days. Is that so?'

'Yes.' She tilted her chin. 'I haven't let you down. We found the plane.'

'You found the plane.' He shrugged. 'That is not important. Not as important as seeing you——'

'I want you to go away,' Kim said in a low voice.

'No. Is it because you saw Jeanne and me——'

'I don't want to talk about it.'

'I do. This may be an ungentlemanly thing to say, but I was *not* kissing her. *She* was kissing me. There is a difference. I don't love Jeanne, I don't even like her. When you came into the room I was holding her arms, trying to stop her. I knew you had seen. I don't love her. I have never loved any woman before. Until—now.'

Kim looked up at him. 'What do you mean?' She had gone calm, icily cold. It was almost as if all this was happening to two other people. Not them.

'Do you want me to go down on my knees and tell you that I love you?' He wasn't smiling—yet. But he didn't look so grim either.

'I—I don't think you're very funny——' she began. She was feeling faint.

'Kim, I am not trying to be funny. I am deadly serious. I have never been more serious in my life. Do you not know how important the search in the lake was to me? Do you think I would leave it now, when it is almost complete—when Gordon and I have everything ready? Yet I have. I am here. Because you ran away from me.'

Kim closed her eyes. 'I think I'd like to sit down,' she said.

'Your grandmother is very kind and thoughtful. She showed me the coffee percolator and put it on just before she went out—about five minutes before you came in. May I make you a cup of coffee?'

'No, I'll do it. I can't let you——' She wondered, as she walked out to the kitchen, why Rinty hadn't been growling. He didn't like strange men, not at all. Yet here he was, welcoming Kim home, waiting with a stranger in the living room, and not growling at all. Not making a sound. How strange, she thought.

'Let me do it—please.'

'No—I——' she stood by the cooker, and her arms started to tremble, and then her whole body. And she wanted Bryce to take her in his arms. She wanted it desperately. She half turned, and the appeal, the longing, was all there in her wide eyes. 'Bryce,' she said. 'Bryce.'

He looked down at her, tall, strong, standing just a foot away. 'I swore I would never touch you again,' he said quietly. 'Do you remember?'

'Yes, I remember.'

'I shall not do so—unless you ask me to.'

'Take me in your arms. Please, Bryce.'

Then he smiled. For the first time since coming into her home, he smiled—and reached out to take Kim to him. 'I love you, Kim,' he said softly. 'I always will. Do you love me?'

'Yes.'

'Then that is all that matters. Will you marry me?'

'Yes.'

'We will live wherever you want. Austria—England—anywhere, you agree?'

'Yes.'

'Is that all you can say?' he said, wondering, smiling broadly.

'No. But there've been so many things—there's so much to explain—about us——' she faltered, because his eyes were so dark and soft—and gentle that she could scarcely bear it.

'Yes, Kim,' he said quietly, 'there *is* a lot to explain—but we will have all the time in the world to do so, do you not agree?'

'Yes. Can I ask you something?'

'Anything!'

'Will you kiss me?'

The coffee bubbled and boiled, but they never heard. Rinty walked quietly out of the kitchen, into the hall, and sunk his head in his paws as he sprawled full length to await the arrival of his mistress. There was no understanding humans at all.

EACH MONTH –
FOUR GREAT NOVELS

Here are the Latest Titles:

Have you missed any of these . . .

Harlequin Presents..

All books listed are available at **95c each** at your local bookseller or through the Harlequin Reader Service.

TO: HARLEQUIN READER SERVICE, Dept. N 512
      M.P.O. Box 707, Niagara Falls, N.Y. 14302
      Canadian address: Stratford, Ont., Can. N5A 6W4

☐ Please send me the free Harlequin Romance Presents Catalogue.

☐ Please send me the titles checked.

I enclose $................ (No C.O.D.s). All books listed are 95c each. To help defray postage and handling cost, please add 25c.

Name ....

Address ....

City/Town ....

State/Prov. .... Postal Code...................

Have you missed any of these . . .

Harlequin Presents..

All books listed 95c

Harlequin Presents novels are available at your local bookseller, or through the Harlequin Reader Service, M.P.O. Box 707, Niagara Falls, N.Y. 14302; Canadian address: 649 Ontario St., Stratford, Ontario N5A 6W4.